PUKAWISS
THE OUTCAST
JAY JORDAN HAWKE

Harmony Ink

Published by
Harmony Ink Press
5032 Capital Circle SW
Suite 2, PMB# 279
Tallahassee, FL 32305-7886
USA
publisher@harmonyinkpress.com
http://harmonyinkpress.com

Pukawiss the Outcast
© 2014 Jay Jordan Hawke.

Cover Art
© 2014 Anne Cain.
annecain.art@gmail.com
Cover content is for illustrative purposes only and any person depicted on the cover is a model.

ISBN: 978-1-62798-646-5
Library ISBN: 978-1-62798-648-9
Digital ISBN: 978-1-62798-647-2

Printed in the United States of America
First Edition
January 2014

Library Edition
April 2014

For Mom.

ONE

JOSHUA RODE shirtless on his skateboard up the sidewalk to his dilapidated home in Eagle River, Wisconsin. He was covered in sweat, but he felt surprisingly invigorated. It was a cool eighty-five degrees out, and Joshua had been skateboarding with his friends at the local park for most of the day. He had only been out of school on summer break for one week, but already it felt to Joshua like it had been a whole summer. Joshua was skilled at enjoying every moment of his free time.

As he approached his front door, Joshua noticed the porch light to his house was off, although the lights in his living room were on. He thought that was odd, as his father always turned the outside light on at 7:30 p.m., even though it didn't get dark till after 9:00 p.m. One could set a clock by his father's obsessive adherence to routine.

Joshua peeped through the door window and saw his mother in the living room watching television. She was uncharacteristically quiet. Joshua's mother was not the type to watch TV peacefully. She was the kind who commented loudly on everything that was happening, typically in a morally judgmental tone. It got to the point that Joshua didn't like to watch TV with his family anymore. He spent his time at night in his bedroom reading, while playing music to mask his mother's relentless moaning.

But now his mother was just sitting there on the couch, as quiet as a mouse. Joshua reasoned that his father simply wasn't feeling well and had gone to bed early. That would explain the lights being on and his mother's apparent calmness.

It wasn't unusual for Joshua's father to get sick. He drank all the time. Joshua could scarcely remember a time in his life when his father didn't have a beer in his hand. No one used the word "alcoholic" in Joshua's home to describe his father's habit. To Joshua, an alcoholic was someone who drank themselves into a stupor, lost all inhibitions, and then beat their subordinate family members violently. Joshua knew families like that. It was all too common in the poor neighborhood he lived in. But Joshua's father had never beaten him or his mother. And neither ever felt subordinate to him. Joshua viewed him as a good man—if somewhat flawed. In his relatively few moments of sobriety, Joshua's father always tried to spend some real quality time with Joshua. He even treated Joshua as an equal, as though they were friends.

If Joshua's relationship with his father was that of equals, things were quite different with his mother. She was the dominant one in their family. She made all the decisions, and she ended all the arguments. Joshua's father rarely argued with his mother. It was pointless. His father always backed down and let Joshua's mother have her way. It wasn't as though his father agreed with his mother on everything—or even on anything. It was more like his father no longer had any fight left in him. He was broken and dispirited and no longer cared. And so he drank.

Joshua realized he would need a really good excuse for coming home so late. His mother didn't like him to be out after 7:00 p.m., even in the summer with no school. Joshua had forgotten to take his watch with him when he left that morning, so he didn't know the actual time. But it was clearly past 7:00 p.m., as the sun was low in the western sky. Joshua had disobeyed his mother, and there would be consequences. There were always consequences.

Joshua could handle punishment, whether it be grounding or extra chores for a week or so. But he would also have to sit and listen to one of his mother's endless sermons first. Those he couldn't handle. They were the worst. She could break the darkest, most malevolent of souls with her sermons—not because she was morally right, but because she was unrelenting. Just when you thought she was done with her tirade, she'd hit you with a prolonged diatribe, wrapped in a sermon, and topped off with a tedious dose of scripture.

Joshua finally opened the screen door to his house and looked cautiously over to his mother. She didn't look back. She had to have heard him enter, Joshua realized, as the door creaked loudly. It always did. But still, there was no reaction from his mother.

"Mom?" Joshua muttered as his mother sat on the couch watching TV.

I'm such an idiot, he thought. She hadn't heard him come in. He could have made it to his room—to his safety zone—bypassing a nightly sermon, but instead Joshua had to call out to her. *What were you thinking?* he scolded himself. But Joshua had to say something to his mother. Everything just seemed wrong somehow, and he wanted to know what was up.

"Mother?" Joshua called again. This time the scolding voice in his head stayed quiet, agreeing that something was wrong. She should have responded the first time, but she didn't.

"Oh, Joshua, sweetheart, I didn't hear you come in," she said gently to her son.

"Sweetheart?" Joshua repeated quietly to himself. Now he knew something was wrong. He had violated his mother's rules, and she hadn't even noticed. And to top it all off, she was being nice to him. This was a true rarity. Something was definitely wrong, Joshua realized.

"They're talking about President Clinton on TV. You should sit down with me and watch," she said.

To anyone else, it would have sounded like an invitation. But Joshua knew there was no such thing from his mother. It was a command. Joshua didn't mind, though. He enjoyed the slight return to normalcy. Whenever President Clinton was on the news, Joshua's mother made him watch. It wasn't because she wanted her son to be informed. She didn't seem to care herself about being informed. She just liked to complain about life. And politics was always the best excuse to do that.

Joshua's mother had been having a field day with the Monica Lewinsky scandal that so dominated the news lately. She always tuned in to get the latest on "that pervert of a president," as she called this particular head of state. Joshua's mother ate it all up. It was sustenance for her soul. She could live on all the hatred.

Joshua sat down obediently on the chair next to the couch where his mother sat. Everyone had their own place in this house. Joshua got the beat-up old chair with torn cushions. His father always sat on the uncomfortable hard wood rocking chair. And his mother always got the entire couch to herself. If you could determine a family power structure by where one sat, then it was obvious who was in charge in this household.

"Today, President Bill Clinton issued a surprising proclamation," the news anchor reported.

"Oh God!" Joshua's mother screamed. "Nobody is watching the news to learn about some stupid proclamation!" she yelled impatiently at the TV, obviously wanting to hear more about the Monica Lewinsky scandal.

Now that was the mother Joshua knew. She was back to her droning commentary now that she had an audience. Things were normal after all, he decided.

"The proclamation declares the month of June to be Gay and Lesbian Pride Month," the news anchor said. The program broke to a clip of President Clinton speaking. "We cannot achieve true tolerance merely through legislation; we must change hearts and minds as well. Our greatest hope for a just society is to teach our children to respect one another, to appreciate our differences, and to recognize the fundamental values that we hold in common." The camera came back to the news anchor, who seemed increasingly uncomfortable with the story. He looked to the camera and sped up his narration, hoping to get that particular segment over with. "'Diversity is a gift,' President Clinton said as he concluded his speech."

"What!" Joshua's mother screamed at the television, suddenly taking an interest in the proclamation. "There is no end to this man's perversion!" she shouted.

Joshua found himself surprisingly interested in the news as well. Joshua's mother had never lectured her son on the evils of homosexuality before, but she didn't have to. Joshua knew exactly where she stood on the issue, as she frequently dismissed President

Clinton as that "gay president." His mother always went ballistic whenever President Clinton said "gay" or "lesbian" in an inclusive way during his televised speeches. The message from his mother was clear. "Gays are bad. Bill Clinton is evil."

"President Clinton's critics view this like his executive order last year banning discrimination in federal employment, seeing it as a run around the Republican-led Congress," the news anchor elaborated.

"So, President Pervert thinks he's a dictator now," his mother mumbled.

Joshua was getting very uncomfortable with his mother's commentary. He was used to ignoring her whenever she forced him to watch the news. But as he was getting older, Joshua increasingly realized he had some major disagreements with his mother regarding political issues. He didn't know anything about budgets, social security, and Bosnia, or even really important things like the Monica Lewinsky scandal, but he knew something about gay people. He could never tell his mother why he knew about gay people, though. So Joshua just sat there silently as his mother trashed President Clinton. By extension, she was trashing her own son as well, albeit unknowingly.

"This isn't the first time President Clinton has been criticized for his advocacy of gay rights," the news anchor stated. "His controversial presidency started off when he tried to lift the ban on gays serving in the military. A conservative backlash forced him to sign the Don't Ask, Don't Tell compromise and later the Defense of Marriage Act. With this proclamation, the president seems to be returning to his roots."

Joshua's mother angrily got up and shut off the television. "Can you believe that guy?" she asked rhetorically. She wasn't expecting an answer. And she never got one from Joshua. He knew better than to answer her rhetorical questions. But this time was different.

"Maybe it's the whole Constitution thing," Joshua said quietly, but with an argument in his voice. "You know?" he continued. "All men are created equal."

Anyone listening to the conversation would not have picked up on the sarcasm in Joshua's voice. He was skilled at hiding it. It's what allowed him to survive his mother's numerous tirades with some dignity still intact. But his mother seemed to detect it this time. *Perhaps I overdid it*, Joshua thought.

"What did you say to me?" she asked, as if not believing her ears.

"Nothing, Mother," Joshua said with another hint of sarcasm. "He's such a pervert," he added, unsure whether or not the sarcasm was still showing.

Joshua's mother had a look of horror on her face, as though her son had been possessed by some kind of demon. The rage seemed to build up in her like a volcano just prior to an eruption. *This was going to be some sermon*, Joshua realized. He had only one option—change the subject and hope it worked. Next to subtle sarcasm, changing the subject was his second greatest skill.

"Let me tell you something about queers," his mother said as she began her sermon.

"Mom, where's Dad?" Joshua interrupted, sounding genuinely concerned. He really was concerned about his father, despite the fact that his question was meant as a diversion.

The impending volcano suddenly fell silent. A look of sadness, even pity, overcame Joshua's mother. He had never seen that expression on her before. He didn't know how to interpret it. He just knew that something was very wrong.

"Mom, is something the matter with Dad?" he asked, concerned.

"We need to talk," his mother finally responded, breaking the awkward silence. "There are going to be some—" She paused to find the right words before finishing. "—changes."

"Changes? What do you mean?" Joshua asked. "What happened to Dad!"

"Your father left us," she said. "He won't be living here anymore."

Joshua couldn't believe it, and yet, at the same time, it wasn't much of a surprise. All his mother and father ever did was argue. Or rather, his mom yelled at his dad, while his dad sat there and listened. Yet that's the way it had always been. It was normal. Joshua was used to it, and now that was going to end. It was too much. Apparently it was too much for his father as well.

"Where is he? Did he leave a message for me?"

Joshua's mother ignored his questions. She seemed lost in thought.

"Mom, where is—"

"Joshua, you're moving," his mother said, interrupting him.

This was too much for Joshua. His life had completely transformed in just a little over thirty seconds. His father was gone, and now they were moving.

"What? Moving? Mom, I don't understand. Where are we going?"

"No, Joshua, not 'we.' You."

"You mean I'm going to live with Dad?" he asked, confused.

"No, you're moving to the reservation. You're going to live with your grandfather."

Grandfather? It was a word Joshua had forgotten. He barely remembered his grandfather. Some of his earliest and best memories were on the reservation in northern Wisconsin. But those memories seemed like a distant dream. Joshua hadn't seen his grandfather in years. There had been a "falling out," as his mother liked to put it. He had never gotten a better explanation than that. And now he was being told that he was going to be living with this man he could barely remember—the father of his father, who had just left him.

"Can I bring my skateboard?" Joshua asked. He knew it was a dumb question and probably even an insensitive one. But if his life was going to change, he wanted to hang on to something familiar—an object, a routine, anything. As long as he had his skateboard, things would be fine.

"No!" his mother said, obviously not in the mood for insensitivity. "Now start packing."

"What a great way to turn fourteen," Joshua grumbled.

TWO

Joshua gazed out the car window at the majestic forests that dominated the small country road on the way to the reservation. He was surrounded by such forests at home, but the mystique of the reservation made the forests seem more alive and magical. The reservation was only about an hour away from his home in Eagle River, but to Joshua it might as well have been overseas in some strange and foreign land.

Joshua's mother had not allowed the family to visit the reservation in years. They used to visit when he was much younger, but that had ended years ago. Joshua couldn't even remember how old he was the last time he had been there. His mother changed the subject whenever he brought it up until Joshua finally learned simply not to talk about it anymore.

Joshua had some memories of the reservation, but they were dreamlike, as though they never really took place. He had disjointed images of some people he had known from there as well. His grandfather was one of them. In his mind, Joshua remembered a very gentle old man with long black hair—grayish in spots. He recalled his grandfather looking down at him, and he was always smiling. Joshua remembered his emotions more than any images, though. Specifically, he remembered feeling loved.

But as the visits to the reservation stopped, and Joshua got older, those feelings faded. His grandfather stopped talking to him at some point. The love must have been a fiction, Joshua reasoned. Whatever falling out his grandfather had with his mother and father, that argument apparently was more important to his grandfather than Joshua was. If his grandfather abandoned him, his love couldn't have been that real. Joshua didn't like the logical implications of those thoughts. After all, his father had just abandoned him as well. *Like father, like son,* he decided.

All Joshua really knew was that his mother was the only person who was there for him right now. With all her faults—all her judging—she was the only one he had left. But, of course, now she seemed to be abandoning him as well. She was driving him to a strange land, to drop him off with a strange man, who had abandoned him as a child. Apparently, he was a man so contemptible that Joshua's mother had not spoken with him for years. And now, she was going to entrust this old man with him. Joshua was not feeling the love.

Joshua and his mother had not spoken since they left Eagle River. It had been a dreadfully quiet and awkward drive. But as they approached the only real town on the reservation, his mother suddenly tried to make conversation with him.

"This isn't forever, you know," she said, obviously detecting that he was upset. "I just need some time to…." She paused to consider her words before continuing. "I need some time to sort things out. That's all."

"Why can't you sort things out with me in the house?" Joshua asked sarcastically. "You didn't even let me say bye to my friends." His tone changed quickly from sarcasm to accusatory. He had always been good at that.

"I thought it would be best not to drag things out," she responded. "And you couldn't stay at the house because I'm not going to be there."

"What?" Joshua said, confused and concerned. "Where are you going?"

"Home," his mother said. "I'm going home."

Joshua didn't understand. She had no home, not really. Her mother's parents passed away years ago. Joshua had never even known them. He knew that his mother grew up in Rockford, Illinois, many hours south of Eagle River, but he had never been there. Without her family to visit, Joshua figured his mother never felt any reason to go back there. But maybe he was wrong. Maybe she did still have family there—an aunt or uncle, perhaps. Maybe Joshua even had some cousins he didn't know about. Joshua was momentarily excited at the thought. Anything that made him feel less alien to his family, no matter how remote that possibility.

"I'll be staying with my sister," his mother finally said. "And she has a small house and can barely handle me right now, let alone a teenage boy."

An aunt, Joshua noted. His mother had a sister, and he never even knew about it.

"Besides, Joshua, this isn't going to be for long. Just until I get settled. So don't be a sissy about this," his mother chided while trying to hold back her tears.

Joshua hated it when his mother did that, although she had no way of knowing it. It wasn't just that she was abandoning him to a stranger and pretending it was for his own good. It was her frequent use of such demeaning words—"sissy," "queer," even "fag." These were the words that dominated his mother's lexicon whenever she wanted to discourage "pouting" from Joshua. Feeling abandoned, feeling betrayed, feeling unloved and unwanted—these were unmanly in his mother's eyes, and she didn't want to encourage those feelings.

As the two drove into town, Joshua noted a sign which read The Rez Café. He knew they had arrived. Another sign next to a dilapidated old stand noted Wild Rice For Sale. He could see neighborhoods of small, old houses to his left and right, in between the occasional run-down business. Joshua soaked it all in. He was only an hour from his home in Eagle River, yet everything already seemed so foreign to him. *So Indian,* he thought.

Joshua considered it odd that the reservation should seem so strange to him. His father was a full-blooded Ojibwe, after all, and Joshua was half that. But his father had never talked about his Native American heritage and certainly didn't teach Joshua anything about it. His mother would never allow that. So all he really knew about being Indian was what he learned in books. The public library in Eagle River was practically a second home for Joshua. He did everything to avoid his awkward home life, and when he wasn't out skateboarding with his friends or running, he loved to read at the library. It helped that he could get the latest music CDs there as well, which is what he always told his friends he was doing.

Joshua spent many hours at the library going from one section to the next, from nature books about plants and geology, to astronomy and history. But he also occasionally picked up a book about Native Americans. Very little from those books stuck with him, though. He read books about Native American mythology, and it all just seemed too *Harry Potter* for him.

Harry Potter, that's it! Joshua realized. He had just finished reading that novel. Everyone was talking about it, and he understood why. It was truly magical. Joshua now realized that was how he saw all the books he read about Native Americans. It was like reading about some strange world where mythological creatures coexisted neatly with magic and humans.

But *Harry Potter* was fiction, and everyone knew that—everyone except these Native Americans, apparently. That's why Joshua never connected with his heritage. It just didn't seem real to him. And so, while he read the occasional book on Native American beliefs, he more often than not went back to books about natural history—something concrete, something he knew to be real.

As they continued to ride through the small reservation town, Joshua next noticed an immense building in the middle of a large parking lot. He initially thought it was some sort of movie theatre. But that was unexpected on such a small reservation. Then he noticed from the sign that it was a casino. Of all his fleeting memories from early childhood, there was nothing about a casino. It seemed so out of place in this run-down town in the middle of an imposing forest.

Why is Las Vegas in the Northwoods? he pondered. He didn't have time to reflect, as only a few moments after passing the casino, Joshua's mother turned the car onto a small gravel road that led back into the woods surrounding the town. Joshua noticed several small, older houses surrounding a medium-sized lake. And after only a few seconds, his mother parked the car in front of an aged ranch home. Joshua was surprised he still recognized it as his grandfather's house.

THREE

IT WAS 4:00 p.m. as they arrived at his grandfather's house. Joshua got out of the car and slammed the door shut. He wanted to make sure his mother understood he was not happy. He walked angrily to the rear of the vehicle and waited impatiently for his mother to open the back car door. He was determined not to say a word, but mentally, he was fuming.

Joshua felt like he had collided with a wall of heat when he exited their old sedan. The car was not air-conditioned, but with the windows open and the outside air blowing in his face the whole way, he hadn't really noticed the scorching hot weather.

Joshua's mother turned the car off and joined Joshua at the back of the car. She was familiar with Joshua's attitude, and she seemed determined to "correct" it.

"If you want to act like a child, fine," she said.

"Child?" Joshua replied angrily. "Are you saying you're abandoning your child?" He knew that would get her, and getting her was all that mattered now.

"I am not abandoning you. I'm simply preparing things. I'm not having this argument right now."

"Oh, now you're preparing things," he said, not ready for the argument to end. "What happened to having to find yourself?"

"That is not what I said!"

"I can read between the lines," Joshua informed her, "even though I'm a child."

Joshua's mother was obviously getting angry. She tolerated a certain amount of talking back when she felt guilty, but her sense of propriety, as well as her ego, could only handle so much.

"Look!" she said. "Life doesn't always go the way we want it to. Mine certainly didn't."

"No shit!" Joshua said, knowing he was crossing a line.

"You just have to man up," his mother responded immediately.

Joshua fumed but said nothing.

"Like it or not, you're staying here with your grandfather."

"I will not like it!" Joshua screamed. It was time for the accusations, he realized. He'd been holding them in. Now he was going to say his peace. "You drove Dad away, you tore me from my friends, you ruined my summer, and you took me from my home! I don't even know the creepy old man you're making me live with!"

Joshua was shocked by his own gall. He had talked back to his mother before, but never like this. His anger had been boiling over, and he finally just exploded. It felt liberating, he realized. But that liberation only lasted for a second as Joshua noticed his mother staring over his shoulder, looking awkward and embarrassed.

Please don't let him be standing behind me, Joshua thought anxiously, sensing his grandfather was there. As he turned around, he was struck by an unexpected sight. Standing behind him was an Indian boy, staring quizzically at the two as they fought. Joshua wondered how long he had been standing there. He was an older boy, Joshua guessed, about sixteen years old. His hair was cut short, except for a very prominent red-dyed Mohawk running down the middle. He had a tall, skinny frame. But Joshua especially noticed his almost hypnotic brown eyes as he gazed back at Joshua.

Joshua's face momentarily turned bright red, nearly matching the odd boy's hair. His emotions instantly transformed from anger at his mother to embarrassment from his own actions.

"Can I help you two?" the stranger finally asked.

"We're just fine, thank you," Joshua's mother said to the perplexed boy. "This is my father-in-law's house."

Joshua felt like he had to chime in as well. "Um, uh, yeah," he mumbled awkwardly.

The Indian boy stared quizzically at Joshua.

Finally, trying to redeem himself from looking like a fool, Joshua said: "I'm, uh, Jah... uh, Josh...." And then he paused as he forgot the rest of his name. "Uh," he finally added after what seemed like an eternity of embarrassment. "I'm such an idiot," Joshua whispered inaudibly to himself. After contemplating how dumb he had sounded, he put out his hand to greet the stranger.

Unexpectedly, the strange boy immediately received Joshua's hand and clasped it firmly. He stared into Joshua's eyes some more. Joshua tried to avert his eyes but couldn't.

"Well, Jah-Josh-ua," he teased. "It's an honor to meet you again, my brother," he added. "Oh, and Gentle Eagle isn't here right now. But he'll be back shortly. I will definitely be seeing you around," he said as he walked back to the house next door.

Joshua stared at him incredulously as he walked away. He got into his car, which was sitting in the driveway next door. The strange Indian boy nodded good-bye as he started the car.

Sixteen, definitely, Joshua decided. After all, this boy could drive, so he must have a license. Only then did the words "Gentle Eagle" emerge from his mental buffer.

"Who is Gentle—" he began to say before realizing the obvious. Gentle Eagle must be his grandfather's Indian name.

"Wait!" Joshua yelled to the strange boy, hoping to catch him before he drove off. "What's your name?"

The boy smiled. "*Mokwa ndishnikaaz*," he responded in words that sounded nonsensical to Joshua.

"Nice to meet you, *Mookwa dish... n... oyz*," Joshua mumbled, attempting unsuccessfully to parrot the boy's peculiar words.

The strange boy laughed. "No, just Mokwa," he corrected. "Ndishnikaaz" just means 'is my name.'"

Again, Joshua felt like a fool.

Mokwa raced off in his car, leaving Joshua behind with his mouth agape. He finally decided to continue the spat with his mother. He grabbed his luggage, which consisted simply of an old, beat-up backpack, from the car. His mother glared at him almost accusingly.

"What?" Joshua asked, "I'm getting my luggage, sheesh."

As his mother watched him get his bag, Joshua unexpectedly realized he was now looking forward to meeting his grandfather. Fourteen was a confusing age, he thought. He could barely keep up with his emotions. A moment ago, he was determined never even to get out of the car, and now he was obsessing over an odd boy he had never seen before. That was an especially difficult feeling to process with his mother standing right there. Joshua had known for a while that his feelings made him different from most boys. He had tried at first to deny that he was gay, but he couldn't any longer. Moments like the one he'd just had with the Indian boy only confirmed it to him. No girl had ever made him so embarrassingly tongue-tied before.

"Joshua, where are you?"

"Huh?"

"You look a million miles away," his mother said.

"Um," Joshua said, trying to focus. "So how long do we have to wait here?" he asked, anxiously trying to change the subject. He couldn't let his mother suspect for a second that he had feelings for another boy. She wouldn't understand. For her, it was taboo—and for everyone else on the reservation, as far as Joshua knew.

"Do I look like I can read minds?" his mother responded. "Of course I don't know when he'll be back. You never know with your grandfather." She looked annoyed, as though she were talking from experience.

"Well, you'd think he'd have the courtesy to be here since he knew I was coming," Joshua said, feeling aggravated.

She said nothing in response. Her silence was a disturbing revelation. His mother always had something to say, as she constantly had to get the last word in. Her silence in this case could only mean she had something to hide.

"Wait," Joshua said, grabbing the luggage in his mom's arms. "He knows I'm coming, right?"

An uncomfortable silence followed.

"Mother!"

"Joshua, your grandfather doesn't have a phone," she said, trying to explain herself.

"Oh my God!"

"Well, now, how could I tell him if he doesn't have a phone, and don't you dare use the Lord's name in vain."

"Great, just great," Joshua said. "I'm surprised you're even waiting here with me. You probably wanted to just drop me off and drive away without even getting out of the car!"

His mother looked even more guilty in reaction to that accusation.

Suddenly, Joshua noticed his mother gazing behind him again, as though there was someone else standing there.

"Unbelievable," Joshua murmured with a hint of embarrassment. He turned around only to see yet another Indian watching the two of them fight. This time it wasn't a sixteen-year-old boy. This time it was an older man with long, black, graying hair.

"Catherine?" the strange man finally asked, breaking the silence. He said the name as though he had just seen a ghost, or as though he thought seeing a ghost was more likely than seeing Joshua's mother.

Joshua looked over to his mother. The two obviously knew each other. This must be his grandfather.

"Gentle Eagle," Joshua's mother said back, acknowledging the man. Joshua detected some bitterness in her response. She was obviously trying to suppress it, but he knew his mother too well.

"I can't say I was expecting you," the old man said as if in a mental fog.

Joshua's mother looked embarrassed, something he immediately picked up on. He never knew what had happened between his mother and grandfather, but it was probably his mother's fault, he decided. Joshua had never seen his mother look embarrassed before, and she never admitted to making mistakes. But guilt was written all over her face.

"I was hoping you could...," she said slowly, stumbling for words. "I mean, there is a problem that—"

"Is it Black Raven? Is he okay?" Gentle Eagle asked, looking very concerned.

"He's fine. It's just...."

It was his mother's turn to be tongue-tied. He had never seen her like this before. She was always confident and sure of herself. Now she was tripping over her own words. Joshua listened intently. He wanted to hear what his mother had to say as much as his grandfather did. After all, she hadn't even told Joshua what had happened between her and Joshua's father.

"Can we talk over here?" she finally said, motioning for Gentle Eagle to join her by the front porch away from Joshua.

Just great, Joshua thought. He was about to get the "you're too young to understand this" treatment from his mother.

Gentle Eagle and Joshua's mother walked over to the porch. He heard them whispering to each other, but he couldn't make out what was being said. His mother somehow managed to reach a contradictory state whereby she could simultaneously shout, while seeming soft at the same time. His mother had mastered talking like that. Joshua's grandfather remained composed throughout the conversation. He stood there quietly and listened, occasionally trying to jump in with a point.

Suddenly the "conversation" broke off as his mother began to cry. She walked toward Joshua, sniffling, while trying to regain her composure.

"Joshua," she said, with a painful tone. "You obey your grandfather. Everything will be fine. I'll be back as soon as I can."

She wasn't coming back anytime soon, Joshua could tell.

She gave Joshua an awkward, obligatory hug and walked to the car. She got in, started the engine, and drove off quickly without looking back. Joshua followed the car with his eyes. It turned onto the main street and was quickly out of sight. And that was it. His mother was gone, and he was alone.

"Bye," Joshua finally said quietly, signifying the official end to his old life.

Only then did Joshua remember that he was not alone. He turned around toward the porch and saw the old Indian man staring at him intently—the man who was his grandfather.

Joshua glanced back awkwardly. He didn't know what to say. Apparently neither did his grandfather. This was going to be an awfully long stay.

FOUR

JOSHUA'S GRANDFATHER finally broke the awkward silence by opening his front door, inviting Joshua to come in. Joshua said nothing as he cautiously walked by his grandfather, half expecting the invitation to be some kind of trap. He entered the house and was surprised by what he saw. The living room was almost completely devoid of furniture. There was a couch, but there was so much stuff on it that one could barely recognize it as furniture. Like the rest of the room, the couch was covered with clutter—tools, baskets, boxes, and wood fragments. It was like the whole front room doubled as his grandfather's workroom. But Joshua couldn't tell what, exactly, that work entailed.

"I guess this will be your bedroom," Gentle Eagle said, pointing to the couch.

Joshua looked back at him as though his grandfather was making some kind of joke.

When Gentle Eagle looked back without smiling, Joshua knew he was being serious.

"You can put your backpack down here," his grandfather said, pointing to one of the few empty spots next to the couch.

Joshua put his backpack on the floor in the designated spot and then wondered what he was supposed to do next. There wasn't even a place for him to sit down.

"You can move some of that stuff onto the floor," his grandfather said, pointing to the items on the couch. "It's nothing important."

Joshua obliged.

"Oh, you must be hungry," Gentle Eagle said, as if realizing for the first time that he was in charge of someone.

"No," Joshua interrupted, not wanting to sit through an awkward dinner conversation with a strange man. "I mean, we ate right before we arrived." It was a lie, but Joshua saw no other way to avoid the situation.

"Oh," his grandfather said, nodding. "Of course you did."

"If it's okay, I'd just like to read a bit."

Gentle Eagle looked surprised, but he was agreeable enough. "Sure, you get some reading done. We'll talk in the morning."

With that, Gentle Eagle went into his bedroom. Joshua wondered if his grandfather's bedroom looked anything like his living room. He tore his jeans off and lay on the couch in his boxers. There was no pillow, but Joshua rolled up some of the clothes he had stashed in his backpack. Two sweatshirts made for a good enough pillow. There were certainly enough blankets lying around, but he didn't need one. It was too hot for blankets. Then he noted that there was no fan. *This is not happening*, he thought, almost in a panic.

He spent the next couple of hours pretending to read some of the books he had brought with him from home. He realized he wouldn't be able to return any of them to the Eagle River library where he had checked them out. *Mom's totally going to pay the late fine*, he thought.

Joshua couldn't really concentrate. As the sun began to set, he finally put his book aside and just lay there. The day's events raced through his mind. Yesterday he had been a relatively content kid, getting ready for a long day of skateboarding with his friends. Now, he was a stranger in a strange land. He had no friends, no father, no mother, and worst of all, no fan.

He hated it when his mind raced. It usually meant a very restless sleep lay ahead. He'd have to lie there for hours before he'd be able to fall asleep. It took only ten minutes, however, before he drifted off into a much-needed slumber.

JOSHUA FOUND himself in an unusually vivid dream. He was sitting in a birchbark canoe, enjoying the calm of a beautiful blue lake surrounded by the lush green forest. White puffy clouds dotted an enticingly tranquil sky. In front of him sat Mokwa, the strange Ojibwe boy he had just met. Mokwa had no shirt on, and he was gazing back at Joshua.

"Look over there," Mokwa said, pointing above the trees over toward the shore. Joshua could see dark, foreboding storm clouds in the distance.

"We should get back to shore," he said, feeling anxious and concerned.

"Don't worry," Mokwa said back to him. "That storm looks like it's months away."

That was an odd thing to say, Joshua thought to himself. No storm travels that slowly.

"And besides," Mokwa continued, "I'll protect you."

Joshua smiled at that. It comforted him to know Mokwa was looking out for him.

Suddenly, the sounds of Eric Clapton erupted from the surrounding forests.

"What's that dreadful sound?" Joshua asked.

Joshua awoke drenched in sweat. If only he had had a fan. Hot weather always gave him weird dreams. He felt disorientated, not only from being in someone else's house, but from being jolted awake by a loud noise. He yawned and tried to come to his senses. Then he realized the noise was coming from his grandfather's room. It almost sounded like music.

It can't be, Joshua thought. *Maybe I'm still dreaming?* He recognized the music right away. It was an Eric Clapton riff. His father used to play it all the time. Joshua realized his grandfather probably had a clock radio that just went off. He thought he'd better go wake the old man up, or he'd have to listen to that noise forever.

What time is it anyway? Joshua wondered. He could see the sun was coming up, only then realizing he had slept straight through the night.

Joshua got up off the couch. His T-shirt and boxers stuck to his body, as sweat had soaked into his clothes during the night. He walked to his grandfather's room and cautiously opened the door, thinking he'd have to go in and wake the man up. What he saw was most unexpected.

Not only was his grandfather wide awake, but he was sitting upright in his bed with an electric guitar in his hands. It was plugged into a nearby amp, and Gentle Eagle was jamming away at the guitar. Gentle Eagle looked over to Joshua peeking at him from the door.

"How is this for an alarm clock?" he asked. "Hope I didn't wake you," he added, but that was obviously not the case.

"Um, no, I usually get up early," Joshua responded cautiously.

"Good, we'll get along just fine, then," Gentle Eagle said, continuing the riff on his guitar. "You like Clapton?"

"Uh, sure," said Joshua, not wanting to offend his grandfather.

"Your father sure did," Gentle Eagle said. "He could play all of his songs. I taught him every one of them."

Joshua was surprised to hear that. He knew his father liked Clapton, but he didn't know his father played the guitar—other than a few riffs.

"Sit down," Gentle Eagle offered, pointing to the corner of his bed. The bed was already made, which also surprised Joshua. In fact, everything in the bedroom looked neat and tidy. There was no clutter on the floor, and the room even had furniture in it—including a fan.

He does have a fan! Joshua noted excitedly.

"Come on, sit down. I'll play your father's favorite song."

Joshua reluctantly walked over to the bed and obediently sat down.

His grandfather proceeded to play Clapton flawlessly. In fact, it sounded better than any Clapton recordings Joshua had heard. His grandfather was some kind of rock god. That was not what Joshua had expected from the short time he'd spent with his grandfather the previous night. *Maybe this old man won't be so bad after all.*

When Gentle Eagle finished the song, he looked up as if expecting to see Joshua excited. Instead Joshua just sat there quietly.

"Well, if that doesn't impress you," his grandfather said, "nothing will."

"No," said Joshua, worried that he had offended Gentle Eagle. "That was awesome. Really." The words were right, but the emotions were off. But it was too late. His grandfather could tell he didn't like his guitar playing.

"What's the matter?" Gentle Eagle asked. "Don't you like Clapton?"

"Oh, well, yeah," Joshua said, fumbling for words. He was getting tired of not knowing what to say on the reservation. He constantly struggled to form even one simple coherent sentence.

"Go on. Say what's on your mind," his grandfather invited. His father had always pushed him to do that as well.

"Well, it's kind of old school," Joshua said carefully, not wanting to offend his grandfather.

Gentle Eagle sighed gently. He paused for a second as if lost in thought and then burst out in a powerful laugh.

Joshua thought for a second his grandfather was going to have a heart attack. Suddenly, Gentle Eagle stopped laughing and stared deeply into Joshua's eyes.

"Of course," Gentle Eagle finally said. "Now what is it you kids listen to these days? Barry Manilow? No? How about Zeppelin? Madonna? No, still too old-fashioned," he concluded.

Joshua smiled as his grandfather played a signature riff for each artist as he listed them off.

"Hmmmm," Gentle Eagle said. "I think I know what you need to hear."

Gentle Eagle started jamming again on the guitar. Joshua didn't know what to do. His grandfather seemed determined to show off his mad guitar skills in order to impress him. But Joshua didn't really like classic rock.

"I mean, you're really good at the guitar and all…." He paused as he realized what his grandfather was playing. "Oh my God!" he shouted in amazement. An expression of pure delight overcame him. "That's Nirvana! You can't possibly know Nirvana! How in God's name do you know Nirvana?" Joshua realized he finally had his voice back, as he was talking coherently again.

"Because I'm too old?" his grandfather asked, while jamming on the guitar.

"No, that's not what I meant," Joshua insisted.

Gentle Eagle continued with the riff.

"Then say what you mean," his grandfather replied, nearly busting out in laughter again.

Joshua just sat there silently, not knowing how to answer.

"You mean it's young music," his grandfather said. "Don't you?" Gentle Eagle stopped playing and put down the guitar.

"Well, yeah," said Joshua. "That's my music."

"Show me your receipt," Gentle Eagle teased.

This time it was Joshua's turn to burst out into laughter. When he calmed down, he realized that things weren't going to be as bad on the reservation as he'd originally thought.

"I thought—" Joshua started to say before stopping himself.

"Say it," Gentle Eagle challenged.

Joshua just sat there awkwardly, wondering if he should say what he was really thinking.

"I don't really know the rules around here," he finally said.

"Let me tell you something," his grandfather said intently. "The rules are that when you have something to say to me, you always have the right to say it. If you are worried about offending me, you can always apologize. That's why the Creator invented apologies. Now what did you think?"

"I thought there would only be powwow music on the reservation," Joshua muttered, feeling stupid even as he said it.

His grandfather stared at him silently.

Joshua wondered if he had offended his grandfather. His concern melted away when Gentle Eagle once again broke out into uncontrollable laughter. Joshua was instantly relieved.

"Well, you have to admit," he said, "it was a reasonable assumption."

"Reason doesn't always lead to truth," his grandfather said. "But you're right. I do also listen to powwow music."

Gentle Eagle put his guitar down and turned off the amp. Still laughing, though quieter now, he put his arm around Joshua's shoulder and stared deeply into his eyes.

"Joshua, my grandson, you are going to find that a lot of things on the Rez are not what you expected."

Joshua stared back into his grandfather's eyes.

"Some things will be familiar to you. Others will be quite…." He paused. "Quite Indian."

Joshua said nothing. He couldn't. He just listened carefully and stared back into his grandfather's powerful, yet gentle, eyes.

"But, no matter what, the one thing that will always be familiar is how I feel about you. You are my grandson, and I love you, and I will take care of you the best that I know how. That is my promise. So at least that part of your life hasn't changed."

Joshua felt an overwhelming sense of calm. No one had ever talked to him like that before. It felt good. But at the same time, he knew this wise man standing in front of him could, in fact, make mistakes. Familial love was rather foreign to Joshua, he realized. In fact, it was quite alien to him. He never felt it from his mother. And his father was too dispirited to truly ever express anything resembling love.

"Get dressed, Joshua," Gentle Eagle said. "We need to get you some food."

"Where are we going?" Joshua asked.

"The Rez Café. If you're going to live on the Rez, you might as well enjoy traditional Native American cuisine."

Joshua's thoughts ran wild. *What is traditional Native American cuisine?* Thoughts of deer sausage and raccoon soup ran through his mind. He wasn't ready for that.

Gentle Eagle looked at him oddly, revealing he understood that Joshua likely had stereotypes about Native American food.

"Relax, my grandson. We're talking pancakes and eggs here."

Joshua smiled. He was starving, and pancakes and eggs sounded just perfect to him.

Gentle Eagle put his hand on Joshua's shoulder, and they walked out the door.

"Besides, you'll get the raccoon intestines for dinner," his grandfather joked.

Joshua looked at his grandfather and laughed. Then he stopped for a second, as if lost in thought.

"Wait, you're joking, right?"

"Ha, come on, follow me," his grandfather responded, not answering the question.

The two walked out the door.

"Right?" Joshua repeated as they got into his grandfather's car and drove to the Rez Café.

FIVE

JOSHUA QUICKLY got out of the car after it pulled up to the Rez Café. He immediately detected the characteristic aroma of fresh pancakes coming from inside, and he began to salivate. It was a very enticing odor to a fourteen-year-old boy who hadn't eaten since lunchtime the day before. Normally, Joshua was cautious about new situations. But in this case, he couldn't contain himself. He ran all the way up to the front door of the restaurant, only then realizing his grandfather was still getting out of the car.

"Come on, Grandfather!" Joshua called out excitedly.

Gentle Eagle seemed amused. "You remind me of your father when he was your age," he said while picking up his pace a bit.

Even more enticing odors hit Joshua as he entered the Rez Café. Pancakes were the predominant smell, but he could also make out the alluring aroma of fresh coffee, eggs, and sausage as well. Pancakes were all that mattered right now, though.

He instinctively headed toward one of the tables next to the window, but he noticed his grandfather was heading for the counter. It was obviously his spot.

"Gentle Eagle!" an older couple called out as Joshua and his grandfather walked to the counter. Gentle Eagle nodded back to them, acknowledging their greeting with a smile.

"*Boozhoo*, Gentle Eagle," another man said, sitting at a table next to the first couple.

"*Boozhoo*," Gentle Eagle returned.

It was a strange word to Joshua, yet familiar-sounding at the same time. It conjured up distant, deeply buried recollections from his youth. He thought for a brief moment that he could remember hearing the word as a child. But he couldn't remember what it meant. *It must be a greeting of sorts*, he reasoned from the context.

"Gentle Eagle!" the waiter at the counter said. He had a big smile on his face, as though a close family member had just walked in.

"Good to see you, Smiling Squirrel," Gentle Eagle said.

"And you," Smiling Squirrel said with a big grin, looking straight at Joshua. "You must be Joshua." He extended his hand, and Joshua shook it cautiously.

"How did you know my name?" he asked suspiciously.

"I never forget a face," Smiling Squirrel said.

Joshua thought that was odd. When had Smiling Squirrel seen him before? Perhaps this man knew him when he was a child.

"So what'll it be?" Smiling Squirrel asked, snapping Joshua out of his daydream.

"Pancakes!" he said without looking at the menu. Gentle Eagle and Smiling Squirrel both chuckled.

"Make that two," his grandfather said.

"Boozhoo, Gentle Eagle!" a woman called from the door as she walked into the cafe.

Gentle Eagle looked back at her and smiled.

It finally struck Joshua that his grandfather was a celebrity of sorts. Everyone knew and greeted him. *Perhaps he's the chief or something*. He was too hungry to give it any further thought. All he could think about now was pancakes.

"I used to take your father here when he was younger," Gentle Eagle said.

Joshua nodded, indicating he'd heard, but he said nothing in response. He didn't want to talk about his father, not now.

"Your father also liked pancakes."

"Small world," Joshua said sarcastically.

Gentle Eagle simply nodded. He had to have gotten the hint, Joshua thought.

"You know, he was about your age when—"

"Grandfather," Joshua interrupted. "Dad left me without saying a word. I don't really care that he liked pancakes."

Joshua regretted his irritable tone the moment the words came out of his mouth. Gentle Eagle seemed like a nice man, and whatever his father did to him, his grandfather certainly wasn't to blame. Furthermore, Joshua knew this man was sincerely trying to help. He didn't make that any easier by giving his grandfather attitude. But the sense of betrayal had been boiling up in him since his mother told him his father had left. Those feelings had been bound to surface, and his grandfather just happened to be in the way when they did.

"I'm sorry," Joshua said. "I didn't mean to—"

"No," Gentle Eagle interrupted. "You have a right to your feelings. When you are ready to talk about it, we will talk. If you are never ready, then we can just eat pancakes."

"It's a deal," Joshua said with a smile, relieved that his grandfather understood.

Smiling Squirrel arrived with a big stack of pancakes and placed them in front of Joshua, who could barely contain himself. He grabbed his fork and dug in.

"Don't forget to chew," Smiling Squirrel joked.

Joshua gulped down a big mouthful. Just then a small piece got stuck in his throat, and he began to cough. Tears quickly welled up in his eyes.

"Are you okay?" Gentle Eagle asked, concerned.

Joshua couldn't answer as he instinctively gasped for air. He turned around and coughed loud enough to stop the conversations of everyone in the room. A small lump of pancake flew from his mouth and splattered onto a young man standing behind him.

"You eat too fast," Mokwa said as he wiped the pancakes off his shirt.

"They always forget to chew," Smiling Squirrel noted.

Joshua's face turned bright red.

"I'm soh… wry," Joshua let out, recovering from his coughing spree. He reached for a glass of water. But in trying to regain some composure, he swallowed the water too quickly. Again he coughed, this time spraying water from his mouth like a massive geyser.

Mokwa looked down at his shirt. It was drenched from the spray. Joshua had never felt so embarrassed in his entire life.

"It's hot out, but I can manage on my own," Mokwa teased.

Joshua smiled, not knowing what else to say. He had humiliated himself in front of Mokwa twice now. *Stupid idiot*, he chastised himself. He was now more determined than ever to keep his composure for the rest of the conversation. He simply ceased all activity. He said nothing, ate nothing, and drank nothing.

"Gentle Eagle, I forgot to pick up the water jugs in front of your house. I'll go back and get them and meet you at the village. We'll need them today."

"Yeah," Gentle Eagle agreed, "it's supposed to be another scorcher." He looked to Joshua, who was sitting quietly. "I hope you enjoyed the pancakes, because it's almost time for work."

That caught Joshua by surprise. He didn't realize his grandfather had a job, let alone that Joshua would be there working with him. He wondered what his grandfather did for a living. He hadn't seen many businesses on the reservation. Perhaps his grandfather worked at the casino. Joshua could have simply asked, but he was worried about saying something dumb in front of Mokwa. So, he just looked at his grandfather and said nothing.

Mokwa gazed at Joshua as he sat there quietly. "Well, Jah-Josh-ua, I will see you soon."

Joshua looked back at Mokwa.

"Oh, by the way," Gentle Eagle said to Joshua, "Mokwa will be your mentor."

Don't say anything, repeatedly played in Joshua's mind like a skipping record. "Well, see you soon, Mookwa *ndishnikaaz*," Joshua said, trying to make a joke.

Mokwa smiled awkwardly.

"Just Mokwa," he reminded Joshua.

"Oh, I know," Joshua said, feeling embarrassed. "I was just kidding."

"I know you were. So was I," Mokwa said. He smiled and walked out.

Joshua again felt stupid. But at the same time, he felt pure elation. *What is wrong with me?* He couldn't think straight. No boy had ever had this effect on him before. Of course, no boy Joshua had ever known sported a bright red Mohawk either.

"Boy, that cough was pretty bad," Gentle Eagle said to Joshua. "Your face is still red."

But Joshua knew it wasn't due to the cough.

SIX

AFTER DRIVING on a country road leading into the forest for a few minutes, Joshua and his grandfather arrived at what looked to Joshua like a small village. They had only driven about five minutes from the reservation town, and already it felt like they were in the middle of nowhere. Of course, to Joshua, the reservation town itself seemed like the middle of nowhere. But this was different. It was like stepping back in time.

The two pulled into a gravel parking lot, and Joshua saw a sign which read in big black letters, *Wiigwaas*. Underneath that, it was subtitled: Ojibwe Indian Village. Immediately underneath that, Joshua read: *Beindigain*. It seemed so alien to Joshua to encounter so many unfamiliar words. He was still trying to wrap his mind around "boozhoo." Joshua couldn't fathom what went on here. *Is this where grandfather works?* he wondered.

"We're here," Gentle Eagle said, stating the obvious.

"Here?" Joshua said back quietly. "Where is here exactly?" he mumbled to himself.

"Here is living history," Gentle Eagle answered. "Come on, I'll show you what I do."

Joshua got out of the car and followed his grandfather to the end of the gravel lot. There stood a log cabin with a sign in front announcing simply Trading Post. Joshua was already sweating as he walked to the building. With the high humidity, it felt like it was in the nineties, despite the fact that it wasn't even 8:00 a.m. yet. This was going to be a hot day, he thought.

Gentle Eagle unlocked the front door to the Trading Post and motioned for Joshua to come in. Joshua entered cautiously, not knowing what to expect. As he looked inside, he noticed it was basically a store stocked with everything Native American. As he looked around, he saw Native American music CDs, books about Native American culture and history, and even Native American instruments like drums and flutes. Arts and crafts were especially predominant, with birchbark objects most noticeable. He saw birchbark containers, birchbark chairs, even a full-size birchbark canoe. *That must cost a bundle*, he thought.

He approached the front counter, where native jewelry was showcased. Beautiful beaded handiwork was prominently displayed in a glass case—everything from beaded bracelets and necklaces to bone chokers and vests. The craftsmanship was highly detailed. Joshua wondered where all this stuff came from. Much of it looked like the items lying around his grandfather's house. His grandfather probably made a lot of the items for sale at the Trading Post. If so, Gentle Eagle wasn't just a talented musician, Joshua realized. He was an all-around artist.

"Did you make all this stuff?" Joshua asked, genuinely impressed.

Gentle Eagle laughed. "Well, some of it. The birchbark items are mostly mine," he explained. "I guess you can say that *wiigwaas* is my specialty."

Joshua recognized the word as the name on the sign they had just passed. *So this is Birchbark Indian Village*.

Gentle Eagle laughed at the thought that he specialized in birchbark. "But," he continued, "I'm afraid I'm no good at making jewelry." He looked over the display case. "Most of this is done by people on the reservation. Stay long enough, and you'll meet some of them."

"So this is what you do?" Joshua said, sounding impressed. "You man the store?"

"Ha, only when I have to," Gentle Eagle snickered. "This place is just the entrance." He walked to the front door and motioned to Joshua. "Come on, follow me. I'll show you what this place is all about."

Joshua was confused. Pulling into the parking lot, all he could see was the Trading Post. But his grandfather had implied there was something else.

He hurried to the front door, anxious to resolve the mystery. He forgot for a moment what really excited him about being here, though—the thought of seeing Mokwa again. Mokwa had indicated back at the Rez Café that he was heading to the village. *So where is he exactly?* The anticipation, combined with the heat, was overwhelming. But he tried to keep his cool. He was determined to avoid another episode of spewing all over Mokwa.

JOSHUA FOLLOWED closely behind his grandfather as they walked along on a small mulch trail behind the Trading Post. The temperature dropped immediately as the dense forest shaded them. Joshua enjoyed the refreshing fragrance of the newly laid mulch combined with the sweet scent of the surrounding pines. It revitalized his spirits, something he needed after the difficult transition he had been going through.

The surrounding woods weren't exactly unfamiliar to him. He may have been new to the reservation, but growing up in Eagle River, Joshua was quite used to lush forests. He camped with his friends back in Eagle River all the time. And even when not camping, his hometown was surrounded by woods. As Joshua walked down the mulch path, he recognized many of what he often called his "nonhuman friends"— white ash, red maple, sugar maple, basswood, red and white pine, and blue spruce. Lower down, he noted several weeds such as chicory, trillium, and blood root. And, of course, dominating everything were the white birch trees that so majestically characterized the Northwoods—*wiigwaas*, as his grandfather called them. It had always been Joshua's favorite tree, despite its prevalence and triteness up north. But if the northern foliage wasn't new to Joshua, what he saw up ahead definitely caught him by surprise.

The trail ended at what looked like an actual Indian village from some previous century. Small rounded structures made of birchbark lined the outskirts of a medium-sized opening in the woods. "Wigwams," Joshua muttered, as he looked at the Indian houses familiar to him only from the books he had read at the public library in Eagle River. But what were wigwams doing in the middle of the woods? He hadn't expected to see Indians on the reservation still living in wigwams. What was this strange place that time forgot? He was instantly intrigued.

"This is a recreated Ojibwe village," Gentle Eagle said. "I created this about a decade ago to teach people about the old ways."

Joshua listened intently.

"We made everything here to look exactly like it looked in the sixteenth century, prior to the arrival of the *zhaagnaash.*"

"*Zognish*?" Joshua asked, sounding confused.

"Zhaagnaash," Gentle Eagle repeated. "The white people."

Joshua enjoyed learning Ojibwe words, but he found them confusing. There was no frame of reference for understanding them. And he wasn't used to hearing "white people" referred to as though they were foreigners. Joshua was only part Indian, and he'd never talked about it with his friends growing up. And while his father was full-blooded Ojibwe, he'd never talked about being Indian either. His mother had seen to that. So Joshua wasn't used to seeing himself as Indian and others as white. But that word, zhaagnaash, struck him powerfully. It separated him from a people he had always assumed he was a part of. But now he was Indian. They were whites. Joshua wasn't used to thinking like that. It came with mixed feelings. While it separated him from a once-familiar culture, it made him feel fundamentally a part of this new one.

Joshua carefully examined everything he saw at the site as his grandfather pointed items out to him. Besides the wigwams, there were racks for drying animal hides, fishing traps for the nearby lakes, bows with wooden drills for making fire, and a birchbark canoe, like the one in the Trading Post.

"This is amazing," Joshua said excitedly. "How come there is no one here to see it?"

"We are closed to the tourists on Monday," Gentle Eagle answered. "We use this day to fix things, rotate exhibits, and make new items to add to the current sites. Upkeep is a constant around here."

Joshua could easily see that. A place like this must have an enormous staff. *That must be what Mokwa does*, he reasoned. And many others probably worked here as well.

"I also need the time to make items to sell at the Trading Post. That's where much of the money for this place comes from," Gentle Eagle added.

"It's a good thing you're closed today," Joshua finally said. "No one would want to visit in this heat." Joshua was already covered in sweat. He wasn't sure if it was new sweat or left over from his very uncomfortable sleep.

"It'll cool off when we proceed on the trail."

"Proceed?" Joshua said confused. "You mean there is more?"

"Oh yes," Gentle Eagle said. "This is just the first stop."

Joshua took his shirt off and tied it around his waist. He could put up with standing in the open sun for a few minutes, but this was going to be a long tour, he realized.

"*Boozhoo*," Joshua heard from behind after taking off his shirt.

"Ha, *boozhoo* to you too," Gentle Eagle teased, recognizing the friendly voice.

Joshua turned and immediately recognized Mokwa. *Oh great, and I'm covered in sweat now.*

"Hey... ah, hi," Joshua said, getting tongue-tied again. "I mean, *boo-jooh*."

"I see you've been practicing your Ojibwe vocab," Mokwa said, smiling at Joshua.

"Yeah, well, not practicing hard enough," Joshua replied, excited that reasonably intelligible words came out of his mouth. "I know *boo-jooh*, kind of, and *Zogni-Zognash* or something like that," Joshua said. "But I'm not quite ready for a conversation."

"*Zognash?*" Mokwa said, looking at Gentle Eagle accusingly. "What the hell are you teaching this kid, Old Man?"

"Just starting with the basics." Gentle Eagle laughed.

"Oh wait, I also know *wiigwaas*!" Joshua added excitedly.

Mokwa chuckled. He looked back at Joshua and said, "Well, you couldn't have a better teacher—or a better school. A few weeks at this place and you'll be an Indian in no time."

Gentle Eagle seemed glad that Mokwa had finally arrived. He probably had a lot of work to do, Joshua decided. He didn't need to babysit some kid he barely knew.

"Mokwa, could you give Joshua the grand tour?"

"The grand tour? That's my specialty." Mokwa put his arm around Joshua and led him toward the trail. "Dang, you're wet," he noted.

"Sorry," Joshua said, embarrassed. "At least it's not from me spitting on you, though."

Mokwa burst out in laughter.

"Come on, Joshua, let's see the world together."

When Mokwa touched his shoulder, Joshua felt like he was going to faint. He was tingling inside. But he said nothing. He knew whatever he said would sound like rubbish, and he didn't want to humiliate himself again. But *wow*, he thought. He was about to spend the entire day with Mokwa. This reservation was truly magical.

Joshua quickly forgot about the heat. All he could think about was Mokwa's arm around his shoulder as the two turned onto the trail to the next site.

"See you, Old Man," Mokwa said to Gentle Eagle.

"Ha, stay cool," Gentle Eagle replied.

"Always cool," Mokwa responded as he and Joshua headed up the trail.

Joshua forgot to turn around and say good-bye to his grandfather. He was too fixated on Mokwa to think about anything else.

SEVEN

MOKWA AND Joshua soon arrived at another site in a clearing in the woods. Joshua quickly noticed two wigwam structures at this location.

"I call this site 'the Indian Skills Camp,'" Mokwa said as he headed for the wigwam. "Let's get things set up."

"Skills Camp?" Joshua said.

"Yeah, this is where we demonstrate the different kinds of skills an Ojibwe needed to know in order to survive."

The two entered the wigwam, and Joshua noted many curiosities. There were small balls stored in birch baskets, and next to those he noticed what looked like lacrosse sticks.

"Lacrosse?" Joshua asked, challenging Mokwa's comment about needed skills.

"Yeah, lacrosse," Mokwa insisted. "And a million other games too," he explained. "After all, how can you live without games?"

Joshua smiled. That had never occurred to him before.

"But seriously, these games helped teach you the skills you needed to track, to hunt, to survive, so that's why we put them in this camp."

"So if this is survival type stuff, do you have weapons here?" Joshua asked curiously.

"Follow me," Mokwa replied, as though he had something cool to show Joshua.

Mokwa brought Joshua over to the weapons area. He took out a key from his pocket and opened a large wooden cabinet. Inside were beautiful handmade bows, with a collection of authentic arrows in a pouch next to them. Joshua also noticed flint stones, presumably for making fire.

Joshua picked up one of the bows and tried to stretch it back. He could barely pull the bowstring apart, it was so taut.

"Careful," Mokwa said. "I'll teach you how to use that someday. But now, we have something more important to do."

Mokwa grabbed what looked like a noose made out of plant fibers and picked up some sticks lying next to it.

"Follow me," Mokwa said as he walked over to the woods at the edge of the camp. "I'll show you how to set a trap." He pointed to the plant-fiber noose in his hand. "The kids love this stuff."

Joshua didn't like the thought of killing animals. He wasn't a vegetarian or anything, but he didn't want to personally hurt a living thing either. He had always been drawn to animals, fascinated by them, both wild and domestic. When he was younger, he used to spend all day following their tracks and observing wild animals in the forests surrounding his hometown. He was especially good at tracking deer. The thought of killing them just didn't agree with him.

"I'm not really sure I'm up for hurting anything," Joshua said, worried that he would offend Mokwa. "Sorry, I guess I'm not much of an Indian."

"*Pukawiss!*" Mokwa explained excitedly.

"What?"

"Pukawiss is a very revered manitou," Mokwa explained. "Like you, he also hated hunting and trapping, and even fishing. His father was very disappointed that he didn't learn the skills necessary to make a 'good' Indian, as you put it."

Joshua was immediately intrigued. "So what did he do instead?" he asked.

"He spent all of his time watching animals and observing them."

Joshua immediately identified with this Pukawiss.

"Then one day he started copying them, and as he tried to imitate their movements, the art of dancing was born. He taught others, and it caught on. That's why Pukawiss is credited with starting powwows," Mokwa informed Joshua. "He is the Creator of the Dance."

"That's awesome," Joshua said, captivated by the story.

"And you are a son of Pukawiss," Mokwa asserted.

Joshua smiled. "I like that." He remembered that Mokwa had referred to Pukawiss as a manitou. "What is a manitou?" he asked, curious about the odd term.

"Manitous are like spirits that inhabit the world," Mokwa explained. "They reside everywhere—in the forests, the sky, the heavens. But some could appear as physical creatures as well."

"So Pukawiss was a spirit?"

"Well, he and his brothers seemed human enough," Mokwa said. "But, yes, he was a spirit, I guess you could say." Mokwa quickly scanned the site before fixating on a nearby structure. "Come on, let's find something that Pukawiss would like."

Mokwa brought Joshua over to the other wigwam at the site. It contained many colorful items of clothing—colored feathers, brooches, chokers, ribbon shirts, loincloths, and trousers. Many of the items resembled clothing Joshua had seen for sale at the Trading Post.

"This is all traditional powwow attire," Mokwa explained. "Much of it was introduced to the Ojibwe people by Pukawiss, according to legend." He offered Joshua a double bustle of feathers. "Here. You look like a Fancy Dancer to me."

"Fancy Dancer?" Joshua said, smiling. "I'm not sure what that is, but I'm definitely not any kind of dancer."

"All Ojibwe are dancers," Mokwa insisted, smiling back. "You don't have to hunt or fish, but if you want to be Ojibwe, you have to dance." Joshua looked reluctant as Mokwa reached out for him. "Come on," he said, "I'll teach you."

Joshua had never danced before and certainly not powwow dancing. He was worried he would look foolish. But he couldn't disappoint Mokwa again, especially after having refused to try the snare trap. *When in Rome*, Joshua thought.

"Okay, let's do this," Joshua said, feigning confidence. "We're about to see how good of a teacher you are."

"All right, watch this," Mokwa said. "I'm going to give you the crash course. I'm going to teach you the very basics of powwow dancing."

Joshua watched attentively.

"First of all, stand like this." Mokwa positioned his legs together, about one foot apart. "This is a two-step dance," he informed Joshua. "Put your right foot forward, tap the ground twice with your front foot, and then pull your left foot forward to meet it—then double step the same way. Simply repeat this as you progress around the dance arena."

Joshua tried to imitate Mokwa, but he lost the rhythm. When Mokwa performed it, his dance flowed and looked natural. Joshua felt awkward and strained as he tried to double tap.

"Like this?" he asked, already knowing the answer.

"You're thinking about it," Mokwa said. "You've got to just do it."

Joshua got a little too ambitious, trying to start a double step with his left foot when he hadn't yet finished the one on his right. He tripped and fell to the ground.

Mokwa simply laughed. "Okay, you clearly need more regalia," he said, handing Joshua a bone choker. "And maybe we need some music. That'll help you find the rhythm."

"Music? Out here?" Joshua asked as he put the choker around his neck.

"Yeah, the beauty of Indian music is that you automatically bring it with you wherever you go." Suddenly, Mokwa began to chant. "*Oh, ah, way, oh ah, way, ya, waayaa way, waayaa way.*" As Mokwa chanted, he double tapped his feet, effortlessly following the rhythm.

Joshua was spellbound as he observed Mokwa's flawless style. He picked himself off the ground, unable to take his eyes off Mokwa. The chant was hypnotizing, and Mokwa seemed to have the perfect voice for it. As Joshua got caught up in a trance, a strong sense of familiarity emerged. For a moment, Joshua thought he recalled having done this before.

"Come on, dance," Mokwa commanded as he repeated the chant over and over. Joshua immediately snapped out of his daze.

Now or never, Joshua decided as he moved to give it another try. The chant helped him to keep rhythm, and he soon realized he was doing it right. His moves flowed almost effortlessly. His anxiety and tension melted away. It felt so natural.

Mokwa stopped chanting and observed Joshua proudly. "You got it!" Mokwa smiled. "And if you can do that, then you can master it all."

"So I'm a Fancy Dancer?"

"Ha, don't get cocky. I taught you some very basic steps, but Fancy Dance isn't just about technique. It's about listening to the drummers, anticipating what they are going to do, and going with it— turning and twisting, bending and...." Mokwa stopped talking when he seemed to notice Joshua's bewildered expression. "Sorry," he said. "I think you learned enough for the day."

Joshua smiled as he handed back the bone choker. Mokwa helped him remove the double bustle of feathers before gently putting everything back in the wigwam.

"Okay, one more thing," Mokwa said as he walked back over to the first wigwam containing the lacrosse sticks.

"I know, follow you." Joshua enthusiastically ran after him and entered the wigwam. Mokwa handed him a lacrosse stick. "I know this!" Joshua said, excited that he finally saw something he recognized. "This is lacrosse!"

"Well, not quite," Mokwa said. "Lacrosse was a boy's sport. This is called 'double-ball.'"

"Double-ball?"

"Yeah, only girls played it. The tourists are always surprised to learn that girls played sports. Come on, I'll show you."

"You're the boss."

Mokwa handed Joshua a double-ball stick, and then Mokwa tore his shirt off and threw it to the ground.

Joshua nearly fainted. It was very hot out and both of them were sweating, but Joshua wasn't expecting Mokwa to take his shirt off. He desperately tried to avert his eyes, but he just couldn't. He was transfixed, this time by the rhythm of his own heart.

I pray he can't read minds, Joshua thought, feeling embarrassed. "So hot," he said as he gazed at Mokwa. Joshua's face quickly turned bright red as he realized he had said the words out loud.

"What?" Mokwa asked.

"Um, I said, it's hot," Joshua responded, attempting to save himself.

"Oh yeah, it's usually not like this till July," Mokwa said. He quickly turned his attention back to the game. "Okay, so here is how you play," he said, handing Joshua a stick. "So, I have the ball." He held up two balls about three inches thick. Binding the two balls together was a leather thong. "You simply hold and throw the ball with your stick by hooking it in the middle of the thong." Mokwa hooked the thong and threw the double-ball to Joshua as a demonstration. To his apparent surprise, Joshua immediately caught it.

Joshua instantly bent his knees like he was about to run forward. He glanced directly into Mokwa's eyes as if daring him to try and stop him.

If Mokwa was caught off guard, it was only for a second. He immediately took the same stance.

Joshua then darted forward. Mokwa blocked his path with his stick, but Joshua pulled a complete 180-degree reversal and went around Mokwa's other side. He darted past, with Mokwa following fast behind him. It wasn't fast enough, though, and Joshua took a clean shot at the goal at the edge of the field. The double-ball flew through the air and smashed into the goal—a perfect score.

"He shoots—he scores!" Mokwa shouted.

"Finally," Joshua muttered to himself. "I got something right."

"Dang, you can run," Mokwa said, seemingly impressed with Joshua's speed.

"I run every morning," Joshua boasted, panting as sweat rolled down his body. "But usually early in the morning—not in the heat."

"Well, you've mastered double-ball. I think it's time for a break."

Mokwa put his arm around Joshua again, even though the two were covered in sweat. Joshua immediately forgot about the heat as Mokwa led him down another path.

"Where are we going now?" he asked.

"You'll see," Mokwa said. "You'll see."

EIGHT

AFTER A few minutes of walking, Mokwa and Joshua emerged on the shoreline of a small lake. Mokwa's arm was still wrapped around Joshua's shoulder, guiding him all the way. A birchbark canoe lay upside down at the edge of a small beach, ready for anyone to use. Joshua caught the cool rush of a refreshing breeze as it rolled off the lake. Two loons noted their presence but continued with their own morning routines.

"It's time to cool off," Mokwa said as he tore off his pants. "Come on!"

"I don't have a swimming suit," Joshua said anxiously.

"Neither do I," Mokwa answered as he removed his boxers. He stood there bare naked for a second while feeling the water with his toes before diving in.

Joshua stood there in a daze, his mouth agape. *Is he doing this to me on purpose?*

"Well, are you getting in?" Mokwa asked.

Not to be outdone, Joshua conquered his anxiety. He tore off his pants and boxers and jumped into the water. After a few obligatory splashes, the two calmed down and began to talk.

"Let me guess," Joshua said. "Traditional Ojibwe swimsuit?"

"Of course," Mokwa said with a smile.

The loons cautiously eyed the two intruders. They finally took off after having had enough of the unwelcome and rambunctious humans.

"Keep up if you can," Mokwa challenged as he darted freestyle across the lake.

Joshua never shied away from a challenge when it came to running or swimming. It didn't matter that Mokwa was older than him, since Joshua was an excellent swimmer. He mentally put aside all thought of his infatuation with Mokwa and focused on beating him. This was a competition, and there could be no room for mercy, Joshua decided.

Joshua dived under the water and emerged in perfect form. Mokwa had the advantage, being several feet ahead of him, but Joshua made up for it with aerodynamics. He kept his head horizontal to the water, pivoting left and right for air. He quickly and effortlessly glided past Mokwa. After about a minute, Joshua noticed the shoreline on the other side of the lake approaching. He stood upright and felt the slimy lake bottom beneath his feet. Mokwa was coming in behind him fast. But Joshua had already beaten him.

"Dang," Mokwa said, panting but sounding quite amazed. "I thought I was in shape, but you are some kind of *nebaunaubae.*"

"*Nebawn eh,*" Joshua tried to repeat before giving up. "Don't even think I'm going to pronounce that one right," Joshua said with attitude.

Mokwa smiled and tried to catch his breath.

"Okay, I'll bite, what's a *nebona-bee-whatever-ma-thingy-jib?*" Joshua finally asked, enticed by the strange word.

Mokwa laughed. "Nebaunaubae," he repeated. "Merman."

"You have mermen also?"

"We have everything! Don't worry, though. In the water, the *mishipeshu* is what you really have to worry about."

Joshua laughed at the obvious joke, and then he paused for a second to consider the comment. *"Mishipeshu?"* he repeated, sounding concerned.

"Follow me, Pukawiss," Mokwa challenged before diving back into the water and heading to the shore on the other side of the lake.

Right on cue Joshua dove in after him. The water felt great, and so did the freedom. Swimming in a lake nude, at full speed, with no one else around—nothing compared to the sense of liberation Joshua felt.

Joshua didn't care about beating Mokwa on the way back, so his strokes were more leisurely. The slower he went, the longer he could be in the water with Mokwa. Joshua wanted this moment to last forever.

NINE

THE SWELTERING heat no longer bothered the two boys as they retired from the lake, drenched from an exhaustive swim. The heat quickly dried them off, but Joshua felt refreshed and reinvigorated. Mokwa spent the rest of the afternoon showing Joshua the rest of the sites at Wiigwaas Village.

Joshua especially enjoyed learning basic survival skills, specifically how to start a fire with flint. Mokwa tried to teach Joshua how to do it with a bow drill, to no avail. But Joshua was a natural with the flint.

Mokwa also took Joshua to a site used for storytelling. He sat Joshua down inside a large long-house structure, which Mokwa simply referred to as "the Wisdom Lodge." There, Joshua learned more about Ojibwe mythology. Mokwa tried to hit upon all the major mythological figures, but Joshua kept bringing the topic back to Pukawiss. He was intrigued by this contrarian manitou. Joshua felt a special connection to him. Even after Mokwa had finished showing him around the village, Joshua kept asking about Pukawiss. The two finally headed back to the Trading Post around 4:00 p.m.

"So Pukawiss was responsible for powwows?" Joshua asked, trying to confirm what he had learned.

"Yes, dancing, singing, drumming, even the colorful regalia so characteristic of the powwow, all of this comes from Pukawiss," Mokwa confirmed.

"And his father didn't approve of his dancing?"

"His father didn't understand Pukawiss. All he knew was tradition. You were supposed to act a certain way," Mokwa said.

Joshua, though, found himself thinking about his mother rather than his father.

"You are supposed to spend your time hunting and providing for your wife and children." Mokwa paused for a moment, then added, "But Pukawiss ignored those expectations for what his father thought were trivial and childish things."

"I feel bad for Pukawiss," Joshua said, identifying with the strange manitou.

"There is a message here for all parents who object to their children going down their own path," Mokwa said. "His father understandably wanted Pukawiss to learn the skills that he needed to survive. And survival skills certainly are important."

Joshua nodded in agreement as he waited for Mokwa to finish his point.

"But Pukawiss went down his own path, and he gave us dancing and celebration as a result."

Joshua finally got it. "You mean he gave them something worth living for?"

"Exactly, *nishiime!*"

"My brother," Joshua said excitedly, immediately recognizing the Ojibwe word.

Mokwa had been teaching Joshua words and phrases all afternoon. Joshua had been relentless in his questioning regarding Ojibwe vocabulary. Every time he encountered a plant, tree, or bird he knew, he demanded to know the Ojibwe equivalent. It seemed to stretch Mokwa to the limits of his knowledge, but he told Joshua he enjoyed meeting someone with such an insatiable curiosity for Ojibwe language and culture. Mokwa worked at Wiigwaas Village because he wanted to share that culture and keep it from dying. But most of his visitors simply didn't care that much. "You are a refreshingly curious student." The compliment only motivated Joshua further.

So all afternoon Joshua picked up new words. Mokwa seemed impressed with how fast he caught on. He repeatedly tested him throughout the day, using words in sentences and seeing if Joshua remembered them. Joshua usually got part of the word right, if not the whole thing.

"Pretty soon I'll be able to keep up with everyone on the reservation," Joshua said.

Mokwa laughed. "Are you kidding? You already know more than most people I know on the Rez."

"Okay, now you're being sarcastic," Joshua muttered.

"No, I'm serious. Many people on the reservation have little interest in the language. That's partly why this place was built and is so important."

Joshua listened intently.

"It's not just to educate tourists. It's to educate Ojibwe as well."

Joshua was surprised to learn that. He saw himself as just a novice, but Mokwa made him feel like he belonged on the reservation.

"So does this mean I'm ready for an Indian name?"

"You already have one, Pukawiss," Mokwa said as he rubbed his hands through Joshua's hair and ran to the entrance of the Trading Post. Joshua smiled and ran after him.

Inside the Trading Post, Gentle Eagle was busy patching a birchbark canoe. At the beginning of the day, Joshua had been surprised to learn that the village closed down once a week to keep things in order. After seeing the entire village, Joshua now understood that patching up items probably absorbed a lot of his grandfather's time. Gentle Eagle even had to bring work home with him, Joshua realized, finally understanding the Ojibwe crafts lying around his grandfather's house.

"I was beginning to think you two got lost," Gentle Eagle joked as the two boys walked into the lodge.

"Oh, if we got lost, you'd find us in no time with your mad *midewin* skills," Mokwa teased.

"Ha, indeed," Gentle Eagle agreed.

Joshua didn't know the word midewin. At first, he thought Mokwa had said "*medawae-idjiwun*," meaning drum. Joshua had learned that word earlier when Mokwa was telling him about Pukawiss and the instruments he had invented. The drum was central to all ceremonies, Joshua learned. But that couldn't be the word Mokwa used in this instance, he reasoned, as it didn't make sense in context.

"What's a—" Joshua started to ask before his grandfather interrupted.

"So, my grandson, I trust you are an Ojibwe now," he teased.

Joshua smiled. "Mokwa is a great teacher! He knows everything!" He tried to bring up his question again, "So, what's a *mide—*"

"Oh, he doesn't quite know everything, just how to get into trouble," Gentle Eagle joked.

"Old Man, trouble always finds me, not the other way around," Mokwa joked.

"So, what's a—"

"Ha, indeed," Gentle Eagle said.

Joshua finally gave up. There would be plenty of time for new words.

"Joking aside, Mokwa, I want to thank you for taking your day off to show Joshua around."

"It wasn't work at all," Mokwa quickly responded as he put his right arm around Joshua. "Joshua is my brother now."

Joshua smiled, while trying to suppress his blushing.

Mokwa walked over to the radio sitting on the counter, which was off. "Old Man, you went all day without the tunes on. Man, you must be getting old."

"If I want tunes, I can play my guitar."

Mokwa turned on the radio. The only station that came in played oldies from the sixties and seventies. The station was from Joshua's hometown in Eagle River, but the reception was great. That station was pretty much it on the FM band. The sounds of Eric Clapton immediately blared from the radio, and Mokwa seemed quite pleased.

Oh no, Joshua thought, realizing that Mokwa was into Clapton.

"Oh man, I love Clapton! He's my favorite." Mokwa laughed as he thrashed an air guitar.

Please don't ask me my opinion. Joshua admonished himself. *Just be honest with him; he won't mind.*

"Hey, Joshua?" Mokwa called as he continued to mimic Clapton's guitar riffs.

"Oh God no," Joshua uttered quietly in a near panic.

"Don't you just love Clapton?" Mokwa finally said, asking the dreaded question.

"Oh yeah, Clapton! I love him!" Joshua responded excitedly, handing over his dignity. *I've got it so bad*, he acknowledged to himself.

Mokwa looked at the clock hanging on the wall and noticed it was after 4:00 p.m. "Oh man, I gotta go. Catch you tomorrow, bro," he said as he ran out the door.

"*Gigawabamin*," Joshua said back, properly utilizing the Ojibwe word for good-bye.

It had been the perfect day, he thought. He had never felt so good before in his entire life. He'd spent the whole day with the cutest guy on the reservation, maybe even in all of Wisconsin, and that guy seemed to like him back. Joshua recalled all the times Mokwa had put his arm around him. And then there was the nude swimming! A perfect day indeed—one he would remember forever. It was the day he fell in love. Life just didn't get any better.

"So what time do we open for the tourists tomorrow?" he asked Gentle Eagle, still beaming.

"Mokwa and the volunteers will arrive around 8:30 a.m. to help set up. We should be ready to open by ten," Gentle Eagle answered.

"Volunteers?" Joshua asked. Up until that point he'd assumed only his grandfather and Mokwa ran the place. But after seeing how big the village was, he realized he should have known better.

"Oh yes, we usually have college kids doing summer internships. Mokwa is my only paid staff. But none of the college interns arrive till next week. So Mokwa is going to round up some local friends to help staff the place this week."

"Oh," said Joshua. "So I guess Mokwa isn't the only Ojibwe expert, then?"

"Oh no, he'll probably bring his girlfriend. She knows almost as much as he does."

Joshua's heart sank as he heard those dreadful words, instantly falling into a deep despair. A rapid punch to the gut would have been preferable. He couldn't breathe as his mind raced to find a scenario in which "girlfriend" meant anything other than "girlfriend." Joshua had never felt so terrible before. This was the worst day of his life. One he would never forget.

TEN

JOSHUA WAS quiet as they drove home from Wiigwaas Village. He wondered if his grandfather knew he was upset. But who wouldn't be? His father had abandoned him, and his mother had pawned him off on the reservation. Not to mention the whole situation with Mokwa. No wonder he didn't feel much like talking.

When they arrived back at Gentle Eagle's home, Joshua crashed on his bed, or rather, on his couch. Despite repeated attempts by his grandfather to convince him to eat something, he wouldn't budge.

"Your mother told me you like peanut butter and jelly," Gentle Eagle coaxed. "You're in luck, because that is one thing I always have plenty of around the house."

Joshua said nothing. He just lay on the couch and stared at the ceiling.

"Or we could go to the grocery store and find some other things that you like," Gentle Eagle offered.

"No thanks," Joshua said sullenly. "I'm fine, really."

Joshua didn't sound very convincing, but he tried to. He didn't want his grandfather to find out what was really bothering him. No one could ever find out. His mother hated gay people passionately, viewing them like some kind of infection. So Joshua knew to keep his true nature to himself. Maybe his grandfather would understand. Joshua entertained that notion for a second before deciding that maybe he wouldn't. It was best simply to keep it quiet for now.

"Okay, I'll make you a deal," Gentle Eagle said. "I won't push you to eat tonight, but you must promise to eat a big breakfast tomorrow."

"Deal," Joshua said, feeling relieved. He regretted that he'd said it rather harshly. He didn't want to hurt his grandfather's feelings. The man had taken him in, after all. And he had been nothing but kind and understanding. He didn't deserve to be stuck with an angst-ridden teen.

"Grandfather?" Joshua called quietly as Gentle Eagle started to leave the room.

Gentle Eagle stopped and turned around to face him.

"Thanks," Joshua said quietly.

"You are welcome, my grandson," he responded. "I'll leave you to your thoughts now."

Joshua spent the rest of the night sitting by the lake in his grandfather's backyard. It contained a small dock with a rowboat attached to it, but Joshua just wanted to sit, watch the water, and think. There was a tall birch tree growing near the lake that provided the perfect shelter for his meditation.

Something seemed familiar to Joshua about that tree. He had been having what he thought of as "emotional flashbacks" ever since he'd arrived on the reservation. Powerful feelings of familiarity kept surfacing in the most mundane of circumstances. After sitting under the birch tree, however, for the first time he had a complete memory. He had been under that tree before. In fact, he had been under it many times before.

Joshua recalled that as a little boy, he used to sit under this very tree for hours. He didn't know how old he was then, but it was obviously before he had moved off the reservation. Despite all the emotional toil of the day, being under the tree helped to center him. He knew he belonged there for the first time since he'd arrived on the reservation. Heartbroken or not, Joshua felt like he was home.

After a few hours gazing at the water, lost in thought, he decided to go to bed. He went inside and crashed on the couch. It was only 9:00 p.m., but Joshua was used to going to bed early. Even his strict mother didn't bother to put a curfew on him, because she didn't have to. He always went to bed early on his own. After a few minutes, he drifted off into a deep sleep. His last thoughts, not surprisingly, were of Mokwa.

JOSHUA DREAMED again of being in the canoe on the lake with Mokwa. It felt so good to be with him. And in his dream, he didn't have to worry about the fact that Mokwa had a girlfriend. He could just enjoy the situation, as though the two of them were all that mattered. Joshua noticed a slightly different element in the dream this time, though. There was a bright red cardinal resting on Mokwa's shoulder. Joshua thought that was very odd, but he didn't want it to distract him from his soothing dream. Yet the dark clouds in the distance seemed ominous, interrupting an otherwise tranquil and carefree fantasy. Mokwa once again tried to reassure Joshua that the storm was months away. *What did it mean?*

Joshua awoke and looked at the clock on the wall. It was 5:00 a.m. It had been a long sleep for Joshua. He sat up on the couch, rubbing his eyes, and wondered what to do next. He felt much better than he had the night before. He still thought about Mokwa, but his thoughts were no longer accompanied by the overwhelming sense of despair that gripped him when he'd discovered Mokwa had a girlfriend. The whole episode already seemed like a distant dream.

Joshua decided to go for a run. He often did that early in the morning back in Eagle River when he got up. Mornings in northern Wisconsin were ideal for running. If you put it off until later in the day, you paid the price. The heat and humidity could be overwhelming. The hot spell they'd been experiencing lately certainly attested to that.

Joshua pulled on a pair of shorts over his boxers and quietly opened the door, not wanting to wake his grandfather. He wanted to check out the larger lake. He could see the sunrise in the distance. A cool breeze struck his shirtless body, and it felt great. He could even smell smoke from the smoldering fires at the campgrounds surrounding the lake.

It was enticing, so Joshua jogged toward the lake. It was only a few houses down the road, so it would only take a few seconds for

Joshua to get there. As he ran past the houses next to him, he saw an elderly Ojibwe lady picking up her morning newspaper.

"Boozhoo, Joshua!" she shouted enthusiastically when she spotted him running by.

"Boozhoo," Joshua called back, unable to mask his confusion and curiosity. He had no idea who the woman was or how she knew his name. As he pondered the first neighbor, he heard another greet him up ahead.

"Boozhoo, Joshua!" a jogger said, coming up on him from the other side of the street. It was a middle-aged woman, trailing a small dog in her wake.

"Boozhoo," Joshua called back to her a few moments after she had passed. *How does everyone know me?*

Joshua reached the lake after only a few seconds of running. He could see tents set up along the lakeside, as well as some campers simply sleeping out in the open. He knew he'd have to be quiet so as not to wake anyone up.

The reservation seemed to be alive with activity at 5:00 a.m., Joshua noted, though it wasn't human commotion. The lake was animated with the morning activities of loons, ducks, and geese. In the trees he noticed sparrows, cardinals, and a wren. Squirrels and chipmunks were especially prevalent as they played, gathered, and otherwise occupied themselves with their morning chores. And most notably, Joshua saw a small fox running along the lake farther away from the campgrounds. No doubt it wanted to grab a quick bite to eat from the local rodent population before the campers woke up.

Suddenly, Joshua heard a strident rattling sound from the trees above. He knew the call well as the sound of a kingfisher, though he couldn't see it. Joshua was good with birds. He could identify many of them from their sound alone, which was a good thing, he thought, since hearing them was often all you got. And thanks to Mokwa, Joshua even knew the Ojibwe word for it.

"Boozhoo, *ogiishkimanisii*," Joshua called out to the kingfisher, relishing the opportunity to speak his new language. The bird frantically flew away, having been discovered by a human. "Okay, bye then," Joshua said.

After about ten minutes of running alongside the lake, Joshua started to head back. He figured that he had run over a mile, and he would double that on his way back home. He felt great, though he was breathing a little heavier. The morning dew, the animal life, and the occasional friendly human greeting him had completely revived Joshua's spirit. He even forgot about Mokwa. Everything was going to be just fine.

"Hey, Pukawiss!" an all too familiar voice called enthusiastically to Joshua from behind. "I see you found my favorite jogging path."

I hate my life, Joshua thought to himself as his heart instantly sank. He felt miserable again. This day was going to suck.

ELEVEN

MOKWA JOGGED with Joshua back to his grandfather's house. All the while, Mokwa maintained his vibrant, amiable, and jovial personality, while Joshua desperately tried to suppress the feelings he was having for Mokwa.

Mokwa seemed to notice that Joshua was a bit glum as he pressed Joshua to open up and tell him what was wrong. But Joshua was determined not to let Mokwa know he was gay—not until he knew him better, at least. So he changed the subject, as he often did, and engaged in the usual banter with Mokwa, pretending everything was fine. When they got to his grandfather's house, Joshua figured Mokwa would go into his own house next door, but instead he ran up to Gentle Eagle's door, opened it, and entered as though he lived there.

"Wake up, Old Man," Mokwa commanded. "I'm hungry." Mokwa slammed the door behind him and walked over to the kitchen.

Gentle Eagle was already in there cooking breakfast, but Joshua couldn't recognize it by the scent. The aroma was mysterious and inviting. He had a keen sense of smell, but his mind had nothing in its mental lexicon by which to identify this meal.

"Yes, master," Gentle Eagle joked back, responding to Mokwa.

The two obviously ate together quite often. Gentle Eagle had told Joshua the previous day that Mokwa was his only paid staff. Perhaps he paid him with food as well as money, Joshua reasoned.

"Sit down, you two. My specialty is served," Gentle Eagle said as he put a bowl of the mysterious dish onto the table.

While Joshua tried to identify the enigmatic meal, Mokwa immediately grabbed the serving spoon and heaped some onto his plate. He had obviously eaten it before. Joshua could make out a few identifiable food items in it. *Cherries, maybe, and some kind of nut— pecans.* The prunes, of course, were easy to identify. The fruit and nuts were mixed in with something dark. *Wild rice!* Joshua was impressed. His grandfather had made a hot cereal from all the things commonly available on the reservation.

"Dig in," Mokwa said to Joshua. "You'll love this."

"You promised you'd eat today," Gentle Eagle reminded him.

Joshua cautiously placed a spoonful of the mush onto his plate. Mokwa and Gentle Eagle stared at him with anticipation. He knew they weren't going to stop until he tried it.

"So what's in it exactly?" Joshua asked before he heaped a big spoonful into his mouth, hoping to placate them. "Traditional Ojibwe meal?" He joked after swallowing.

"Raccoon guts," Gentle Eagle teased.

"Mmmm," Joshua said. "My favorite." He was enjoying the running joke, but he also enjoyed the exotic hot cereal.

His grandfather smiled and sat down next to them.

"Mokwa, did you manage to find any volunteers who will put up with you today?"

"Several, in fact. Even my girlfriend decided that she could bear my presence for the day."

"Any girl who could bear you for that long is a keeper," Gentle Eagle teased.

Joshua thought about rudely asking them to change the subject, but instead his default heterosexual shield kicked in. "So, you have a girlfriend?" he asked, pretending he didn't know. He desperately tried to sound casual.

"Oh yeah, didn't I tell you?" Mokwa said. "Her name is—"

"No," Joshua interrupted, "I'm pretty sure you didn't tell me." He was sure his shield wasn't working properly, as he sounded rather bitter.

"Her name is Jenny," Mokwa said. "And she is sooo hot. She is one very nice dish."

"Okay, whatever, I get the picture," Joshua mumbled. *Damn, I've really got to fix that shield.*

"Well, it's good that you found volunteers. Without the interns, we need all the help we can get," Gentle Eagle said.

"Jenny?" Joshua said in a nasty tone. "What kind of Indian name is that?"

"It's her normal name," Mokwa said. "Everyone on the reservation has a normal name and an—"

"Just seems odd, that's all," Joshua interrupted.

"Jenny was very helpful last time," Gentle Eagle said to Mokwa. "It'll be good to have her back. If we do well this month, I might be able to hire her and make her paid staff."

"She'd love that!" Mokwa said excitedly.

"I'm sure you would too," Joshua accused sarcastically.

"What?" Mokwa said innocently.

"Grandfather, didn't you say there were bears at the village?" Joshua asked, ignoring Mokwa.

"Yes," Gentle Eagle answered. "The whole woods around here have bears."

"What about them?" Mokwa asked.

"Well, I'm just saying. It's kind of dangerous to be in the woods around bears all day. Don't you think, Grandfather?"

"Don't you worry about the bears," Gentle Eagle reassured Joshua. "They stay to themselves mostly. You just got to be careful not to have too much food around."

"Yeah, I bet you could put this crap cereal all around the village, and that would keep them away," Mokwa teased.

"Indeed," Gentle Eagle said. Mokwa and Gentle Eagle chuckled, and Joshua pretended to join in.

"By the way, Old Man, I fixed the—"

"So how long have you and Jenny been dating?" Joshua interrupted, desperately attempting not to say the name "Jenny" with disdain.

"Oh, I don't know. About three months, maybe," Mokwa answered with a smile.

"Oh, so you really don't know her very well, then?" Joshua said, trying to suggest she couldn't be trusted.

"I've known her since the day she was born," Gentle Eagle said. "She's great. You'll like her a lot when you meet her today."

"I'm sure I will," Joshua said, this time not even trying to conceal the sarcasm.

Mokwa was too good-natured to pick up on it, though. That refreshing innocence is what made him so pleasant to be around. But Joshua didn't want to be around Mokwa if Jenny was going to be there all day. He'd had so much fun at the village the day before. Today he dreaded the thought of going there.

"Come to think of it," Gentle Eagle stated, "they did eat one of the intern's tents once."

"What are you talking about, Old Man?" Mokwa said, perplexed.

"The bears," Gentle Eagle responded. "But that's only because I gave them the tents we used for the maple sugaring. I won't make that mistake again."

Mokwa burst out in laughter, but Joshua just sat there with too much disdain to be concerned about some stupid bears.

TWELVE

JOSHUA, ALONG with Mokwa and Gentle Eagle, arrived promptly at Wiigwaas Village at 8:00 a.m. and got out of the car. They headed straight for the Trading Post to get ready for the day. Another car soon pulled into the lot, immediately catching Joshua's attention. The car parked right next to Gentle Eagle's car, and two people got out. Joshua instantly noted that one of them was a girl.

"I'm ready to step back in time for the day," the girl teased Mokwa.

Mokwa smiled back and ran up to her. The two hugged tightly. In fact, Mokwa even lifted her off the ground as he embraced her. "I'm so glad you're here, Jenny," Mokwa said. "We need you so bad this week."

"Gee, thanks for making me feel so welcome," the boy who had arrived with Jenny said.

"Oh my God, you know I love you too," Mokwa said. Jenny just rolled her eyes.

"Come on, both of you, you must meet my new brother." Mokwa brought the two over to Joshua.

Joshua tensed up a bit. He didn't want to meet Jenny. He didn't want to like her. He was going to do everything in his power to make her feel unwelcome.

"Jenny, this is Joshua," Mokwa said. Jenny put her hand out to shake Joshua's hand.

Joshua didn't take it. Surprisingly, he instead put his arms around her and gave her a big, friendly hug. "It's so great to meet you," he said warmly. "I've heard so much about you." Joshua didn't know what had come over him. He wanted to hate her, but he didn't want Mokwa to know that he hated her. If Mokwa knew he hated Jenny, then he would also know Joshua was jealous. And so Joshua overcompensated by showering Jenny with affection. He was so not ready for love.

"Well, whatever you heard, hopefully I can correct it," Jenny joked.

She had a bright and warm personality. Her long, black hair hung on her shoulders and glistened in the sun. She wore a pair of gawky glasses and was a bit overweight, but still, she was good-looking. And she seemed to have a good sense of humor too. *This is not good,* Joshua realized. His mind frantically tried to salvage the situation. *How long have they been together?* He recalled Mokwa saying it had only been a few months. But at the same time he tried to reassure himself that it had only been a few days. *Maybe they will break up,* he decided, as a few days was not very long.

"And this is Jenny's brother, Little Deer," Mokwa continued, motioning to the heavyset kid next to her. Joshua thought that was a strange name for someone so big. But what did Joshua know about Indian names? Little Deer looked to be about Mokwa's age, maybe a bit younger.

Little Deer looked back at Joshua with a stoic expression. He seemed like Mokwa's opposite. Mokwa was always so peppy and outgoing. But Little Deer seemed quiet and wary.

Joshua extended his hand in greeting. Little Deer looked at Joshua's hand, and then slowly clasped it with almost no grip. Joshua did all the shaking.

"Um, good to meet you, Little Deer," Joshua said.

Little Deer nodded back but said nothing in response.

"Little Deer is a bit shy," Mokwa explained.

"Shut up," Little Deer said with no emotion. "I'm just cautious."

"Okay." Mokwa smiled. "Because there is so much to be cautious about here."

"That's what the white man said," Little Deer explained.

"Oh, don't start that again," Jenny said.

"It's true," Little Deer insisted.

"You're part white!" Jenny pointed out, seemingly for the hundredth time.

"That's such a tired argument," Little Deer said.

"See what I have to deal with?" Mokwa said to Joshua. "A crazy girlfriend and her crazy brother—why do I put up with you two?"

Joshua resisted the temptation to repeat the question.

"I know why," Mokwa said, answering his own question. "It's because I love you both so much!" Mokwa gave Little Deer a big, warm hug. Little Deer just stood there awkwardly, not returning the friendly affection. Mokwa turned to Jenny and gave her a much more intimate hug, which she enthusiastically returned.

Joshua thought he was going to be sick. He scanned the surrounding woods to see if there was a safe place to vomit. "Stop those thoughts," he mumbled frantically to himself.

"Seriously, though, thank you both for coming. We are very short-staffed this week," Mokwa said.

"Anything to educate the white man," Little Deer said. Jenny sighed in response.

"So here is the plan," Mokwa said, taking command. "Little Deer, you take the Skills Camp today. You do that better than all of us. And Jenny, well—"

"I know, I'll take the Moon Lodge," she interrupted.

"Good," Mokwa said, relieved. "It's always awkward for a guy to do that area."

"What's the Moon Lodge?" Joshua asked.

"You don't want to know," Little Deer said.

Jenny punched her brother lightly on the shoulder.

"Ouch," he responded quietly.

"So what about you and Joshua?" Jenny asked.

"Joshua is with me today at the Wisdom Lodge," Mokwa announced. "I need to show him the ropes." He paused and looked to Joshua. "That is, if you can tolerate me for another day?"

Joshua was elated at the thought of spending yet another day with Mokwa, especially now that he knew Jenny wouldn't be around. She'd be at that Moon Lodge thing, whatever that was. "Um, I think I can put up with you a little while longer," he said, trying not to sound too enthusiastic.

"Great, it's a plan. I'll see you all back here at noon for lunch."

"It was good meeting you, Joshua," Jenny said.

Joshua pretended he didn't hear her.

"See ya later, Mokwa," Jenny said as she turned toward the trail to the Moon Lodge.

"Definitely," Mokwa said back. "Bye, Little Deer," he called as Little Deer tried to sneak away without acknowledgement.

"Whatever," Little Deer said back, not turning around.

"That kid cracks me up," Mokwa said to Joshua. "He's hilarious."

Joshua mentally questioned Mokwa's sense of humor.

"Come on," Mokwa said, putting his arm around Joshua's shoulder. "Let's get ready for the white man."

Joshua felt good again. It was going to be just the two of them, plus whatever tourists showed up. He could handle sharing Mokwa with tourists. As long as none of them were teenage girls, Joshua told himself.

THIRTEEN

JOSHUA ARRIVED at the Wisdom Lodge with Mokwa's arm wrapped tightly around his shoulder. It was just like yesterday, Joshua recalled as he tried to put Jenny out of his mind.

When they arrived, Mokwa immediately started stripping off his clothes.

"We're not swimming again, are we?" Joshua asked, confused and trying to avert his eyes. He found he was doing that a lot lately.

"No, we're getting into uniform," Mokwa said as he tore off his shirt. "Didn't I tell you about the uniforms?"

Mokwa walked over to a cabinet hiding in the woods behind the Wisdom Lodge. Inside were different types of traditional native clothing. He got out buckskin pants for the two of them, as well as a pair of moccasins.

"Here," Mokwa said, as he tossed a pair of pants over to Joshua. "Put these on."

Joshua stripped down and put on the pants and moccasins. The two were ready in less than a minute.

"Now what?" he asked, feeling awkward in his new attire.

"Now we wait for the tourists," Mokwa responded. "There is plenty to keep us busy until then," he added. "I can teach you how to make a birchbark basket. We always need those. They sell like hotcakes at the Trading Post."

"Okay," Joshua enthusiastically agreed. He would have been equally content if Mokwa had said that they were going to watch the grass grow all afternoon.

"The first thing you need to learn about birch baskets is that we make them incorrectly," Mokwa explained. "Tourists expect the white part of the bark to face outwards because it looks pretty. So that's how we make them."

"Why is that the wrong way?" Joshua asked, thinking that objects should look nice.

"Traditionally they were made with the white facing inwards, since that's the part of the bark that is waterproof. You can't store or boil water if the white is facing outwards," Mokwa instructed. "But it doesn't matter, because tourists only buy them for their looks."

"Yeah, I'm guessing tourists don't do much cooking with these," Joshua teased.

As Mokwa went over the intricacies of building a basket, he was interrupted by Gentle Eagle's voice on the walkie-talkie Mokwa had brought with him. They were perfect for keeping in touch during the day. Mokwa told Joshua that he always made sure he kept it out of sight, so as not to ruin the illusion of a historic village for the tourists.

"Incoming family," Gentle Eagle said over the radio. "*Niiwin.*"

"Nice, we're ready," Mokwa said back.

"*Nawin?*" Joshua repeated.

"*Niiwin,*" Mokwa corrected. "We've got four people coming. Just watch and learn, and you'll be able to do this in no time."

"Do this? Do this! What do you mean?" Joshua asked, starting to panic.

"You didn't think you were going to spend all summer watching me, did you?"

"But I don't know how to do this," Joshua pleaded as anxiety welled up inside of him. He had never taught anything before, let alone a subject he himself was just learning.

"You already know more than many Indians, and that's after only one day," Mokwa argued.

That was a pretty sad fact, Joshua thought. But then he realized that he himself had grown up with an Indian father and had learned nothing about Ojibwe history and culture. Perhaps it wasn't that different on the reservation. For the first time, Joshua truly understood the importance of this mock village and what Gentle Eagle was trying to do here.

Joshua and Mokwa could hear the tourists coming from the Trading Post almost the second they set foot on the trail.

"Tourists are usually very loud," Mokwa said to Joshua. "You can hear them coming a mile away."

After a few moments, a group of four tourists arrived at the Wisdom Lodge. They seemed relieved to find people there waiting to greet them, as though they thought they had gotten lost.

Joshua felt rather self-conscious being dressed up like an Ojibwe boy from the sixteenth century, but the tourists didn't seem to think it was at all unusual. It was as though they were expecting Indians to be dressed like that.

Mokwa greeted them as they entered the area. "Mokwa *nindizhinikaaz*," he said to them. "My name is Mokwa," he repeated in English.

The tourists were mesmerized as Mokwa spoke to them in Ojibwe. They'd obviously never heard anything like it before, and hearing it in the midst of a sixteenth century Indian village, for a moment, aided the illusion that they had stepped back in time. Even Joshua momentarily got lost in the fantasy.

After introducing himself, Mokwa introduced Joshua as "Pukawiss." Joshua got a laugh out of that, but he didn't show it. He was starting to really enjoy that name. Mokwa brought the small group of tourists into the Wisdom Lodge and sat them down.

The tourists seemed a bit anxious, so Mokwa decided to break the ice a bit, Joshua observed. Mokwa started by asking the tourists some questions. He concentrated on the children, as they were always the most receptive.

"Tell me something," Mokwa said to the children. "What is the most valuable life-form on this planet?" His eyes widened as he emphasized the word "valuable."

"Lions!" one of the boys enthusiastically answered.

"No, humans," the older boy challenged, correcting his younger brother.

"Yeah, humans, I guess," the first boy said.

"Okay, humans," Mokwa agreed, going along with the response. "Now, tell me what life-form is the least valuable?"

The two boys looked at each other, perplexed by the question.

"Or a whole category, if that's easier, such as plants, or insects, or—"

"Insects!" the first boy shouted, obviously excited by the hint.

"Yeah," said the second boy. "I hate bugs!"

Their parents nodded in agreement as they started to get into this.

"Good," said Mokwa. "I want to tell you a story about what my people, the Ojibwe people, believe about this subject."

As Mokwa spoke, he moved his head around slowly, gazing directly into the eyes of each of the tourists, as if he was talking to them personally.

"Before I start, I want you to understand that this is a very special part of the village," Mokwa said. "Telling stories for the Ojibwe is not just like telling bedtime stories—something to put you to sleep." He paused for a moment as though he wanted to emphasize the next point. "Storytelling was how the Ojibwe taught their children important lessons—just like you learn at school."

Joshua was impressed. Mokwa had managed to get everyone's attention, including the parents.

"But often the lessons were moral in nature, providing lessons on the right way to behave. So maybe, it's more like going to church," he said, looking right at the children.

"We go to church!" the youngest boy excitedly announced. His mother put her finger by her mouth, motioning for him to be quiet. The boy got the message and immediately refocused on Mokwa's story.

"Usually in the winter, sitting in a place just like this, children like you would listen carefully to their grandmothers and grandfathers tell the stories of their past. In this way, Ojibwe children learned about their place in the world and how they should treat each other.

"The story I want to tell you today," he announced, "is a story about the end of the world."

The two boys leaned forward, intent on hearing every word. A good apocalypse story always got everyone's attention.

"A long time ago, a great flood inundated all the land. Everywhere you looked," Mokwa said, "all you could see was water."

"Oh, I know this one!" the youngest boy interrupted again. "This is about Noah!" He looked at his older brother, expecting him to confirm it.

"Shut up," his older brother whispered.

"Noah, good," said Mokwa, looking at the little boy. "Yes, this is similar to the story told in the Bible."

"See, I told you," said the younger boy to his older brother, looking very satisfied.

"Anyway," said Mokwa, "soon all the animals had no place to go, and they thought they were doomed."

"Didn't anyone build an ark?" the little boy asked.

"No," answered Mokwa. "But they did call out to a manitou for help."

"What's a—"

Mokwa, anticipating the boy's question, immediately explained. "A manitou is a kind of spirit who has great power, but he can look just like a man. And a very powerful manitou, by the name of *Nanaboozhoo*, wanted to save the world from the flood."

The two boys laughed at the name Nanaboozhoo, but they quickly quieted down as Mokwa continued.

"Nanaboozhoo knew what to do to save the world. But he needed dirt as part of his plan. And the only dirt available was deep underneath the water. He asked Bear, the mightiest and most powerful animal on earth, for help. But Bear couldn't help him, as he was powerless in the water. So too was Cougar, and Wolf, and all the land animals." Mokwa paused for a moment, giving the group time to digest this information.

Satisfied everyone was following along, Mokwa continued with the story. "Nanaboozhoo also turned to the birds for help, but they could do nothing. Even the most powerful bird of all, Eagle, could not swim down to the bottom of the water."

"Why didn't he ask Fish?" one of the boys inquired, genuinely curious.

"Well," said Mokwa, "the fish can't hear you under the water."

The boy nodded in agreement, instantly satisfied with the answer.

"So," Mokwa said, "Nanaboozhoo figured the world was doomed. But, then, he saw Otter. He hadn't yet asked Otter for help because everyone thought Otter was useless." Mokwa gazed directly into the eyes of the children to emphasize what he was about to say. "Otter, you see, was considered to be the lowest of the animals on Earth."

"Poor Otter," the youngest boy said, looking like he was about to cry.

"But Nanaboozhoo decided to give Otter a chance, since there was no other choice. So he asked Otter to bring him some dirt from deep underneath the water. Without hesitation, Otter dived underneath the waves and came up a few seconds later with the needed dirt."

"I like otters," the younger boy said.

"Shut up!" his older brother reprimanded him once again.

"Nanaboozhoo then used his manitou powers and blew into the dirt. The dirt magically grew, getting larger and larger, until it was a large island. And soon, it was a whole continent. Nanaboozhoo had done it. He saved the world. But he couldn't have done it without Otter, the least valuable of the animals."

The parents smiled, immediately understanding, and approving, of the morality tale.

"So, what do you think this story means?" Mokwa asked, looking at the two boys for an answer.

The brothers looked at each other quizzically. The younger one offered, "That everyone can swim if they really try?"

"No," said the older brother, "Eagle couldn't swim, and Bear couldn't either."

"So, who could swim?" asked Mokwa.

"Otter!" the two boys said.

"That's right," said Mokwa, "The animal that everyone made fun of—that everyone thought wasn't important—turned out to be the most important life-form of all. And that's why you should never think another animal, or another person, is not important. He may not seem a big deal to you right now, but you never know. Maybe he'll grow up to be president!"

Finished, Mokwa stood up. "And now, it's time for you to go to the next site at Wiigwaas Village," he said, motioning the group to get up and follow him.

The two brothers ran out of the lodge behind Mokwa, followed by their parents and Joshua.

"The trail is over here," Mokwa said, pointing out the way to the Skills Camp. "Another guide will greet you there."

"Don't forget to thank Mr. Mokwa," the mother said to her two children.

The boys immediately turned around, bright-eyed, and as if synchronized, shouted, "Thanks, Mr. Mookwa!"

"I want an Indian name," the younger boy said to his parents as they walked down the trail.

"I'll call you Otter," the other boy replied.

A smile lit up the boy's face as he excitedly tried to keep up with his older brother.

Soon Mokwa and Joshua were alone again.

"You were awesome!" Joshua said to Mokwa, genuinely impressed. "You really know how to handle kids."

"They are a lot of fun," Mokwa said, dismissing the compliment.

"Well, I couldn't have done that," Joshua said.

"I think you'll do just fine, my brother," Mokwa said as he put his arm around Joshua.

"So when are you going to tell me about the Moon Lodge?" Joshua asked jokingly.

"Ha, I agree with Little Deer. You don't want to know," Mokwa said. "Let me teach you some other myths that you can tell to tourists."

"Other myths? Don't you just tell the story of Otter and the Great Flood?"

"Oh no," said Mokwa. "I usually just choose that one when there are children. They need to hear that story the most. But I tell many different myths, depending on the tourists, or my mood. I even tell about Pukawiss."

"You do?" Joshua said excitedly.

"Yeah, whenever I think someone might be gay, I tell them about Pukawiss."

Joshua instinctively tensed his chest muscles, and he suddenly couldn't breathe. Sweat began to form on his forehead, and it wasn't from the heat.

"But I'm not gay," Joshua stammered, sounding defensive.

"Oh hey, relax, man. There are many reasons to call someone a son of Pukawiss. In your case, it's your contrarian nature. You don't like hunting, like I said yesterday."

"But I'm not gay," Joshua repeated, trying to make sure Mokwa got the point.

"You don't have to get defensive, dude."

"I'm not defensive. I'm just saying."

"Anyway, whenever I think someone might be gay, I tell them about Pukawiss, because it allows them to understand the contrast between—"

"You shouldn't call me Pukawiss anymore. People might get the wrong idea," Joshua commanded nervously.

"Dude, if you're going to work here, you can't have a problem with gays."

"But I don't have a problem with gays," he insisted. Joshua thought this conversation was getting increasingly ironic.

"Good, because the Ojibwe traditionally considered gay people to be the most honored members of the community," Mokwa pointed out. "Well, at least, they used to, before Christians came and suppressed it. Thanks to that, many Ojibwe to this day have forgotten about Pukawiss and what he did for the Ojibwe people."

"I didn't mean to offend—"

"My uncle is a two-spirit," Mokwa interrupted. "So you need to get over it."

"Two-spirit?" Joshua repeated.

"Yeah, *niizh manidoowag*. It means two-spirits. It's what many Native Americans call gay people. They were believed to have both male and female spirits. They were considered special, singled out by the Great Spirit. Usually they had very prominent roles in society."

Joshua had never felt simultaneously confused, terrified, and elated. He was confused because Mokwa called people Pukawiss if he thought they might be gay. Did that mean Mokwa thought Joshua was gay? That had Joshua terrified. No one could ever know he was gay. The consequences of his mother finding out would be unimaginably bad. Joshua didn't know what she would do, but he knew it wouldn't be pretty.

Elation was a more difficult feeling for Joshua to explain. Beyond the confusion, anxiety, and fear, Joshua felt like he belonged somewhere for the first time in his life. He had always felt like he was alone in the universe. His mother and father, his culture, his religion, they all rejected him. But now, Joshua realized, that simply wasn't true. An entirely different culture, one he was a part of, one he was getting to know for the first time, embraced him, elevated him, revered him, and most importantly, had a place for him. Joshua wanted to learn more about these so-called "two-spirits."

"Did you say your uncle is gay?" he asked. Joshua had never met another gay person before.

"I hope that's not a problem for you," Mokwa said, as if preparing to defend his uncle.

"Of course not," Joshua said angrily. "I told you, I don't care if someone is gay."

"Then why are you mad?" Mokwa asked.

"I'm not mad," Joshua shouted. He realized he was shouting and lowered his voice. "I just don't want anyone thinking that I am gay."

"Well, if nothing is wrong with it, then who cares? I don't care if anyone thinks I'm gay," Mokwa insisted. "I'm gay!" he shouted out loud. Terrified birds took off from the safety of the nearby trees. "See? No big deal."

Joshua gladly entertained the idea that Mokwa was gay for a moment. Then reality kicked in. "You don't understand, Mokwa. You don't know my mother or my father."

"Oh, I get it. Very Christian, eh?" Mokwa motioned with his fingers to indicate quotation marks when he said "Christian."

"You could put it that way," Joshua said.

"Well, people just don't understand," Mokwa explained. "Sorry I got out of control. I guess I get a little defensive of my uncle."

"It's okay. I get it," Joshua said. "So Pukawiss was gay?"

"Well, I like to think so. Women threw themselves at him constantly as he traveled from village to village, teaching about the dance he had created. But he rejected them all. He loved bright-colored clothing, and they tried to entice him by giving him all kinds of exotic items to wear. But, still, he refused to stay with any of them. All he cared about was his dancing. I think he was gay. It makes sense to me."

Joshua was spellbound. He thought about the stories he had learned at church, and he couldn't recall anyone important ever having been gay. But here in Ojibwe legends was a powerful manitou who may have been gay.

Joshua had enjoyed being called Pukawiss simply because it was Mokwa saying it. But now he was drawn to Pukawiss because it made him feel like he truly belonged somewhere. For the first time in his life, he felt good about being gay.

At that moment, he wanted to shout out that he was gay, just like Mokwa had done. Mokwa made it seem like it was no big deal. But Joshua still wasn't prepared to talk about it. Nevertheless, his feelings for Mokwa increased even more. He had never before known anyone so supportive of gays.

"I'm still going to call you Pukawiss," Mokwa said, interrupting Joshua's thoughts.

Joshua sighed and then smiled. "I guess it's okay."

FOURTEEN

MOKWA AND Joshua arrived back at the Trading Post at noon, just in time for a lunch break. It had been a successful morning. Fifteen tourists altogether had come through the Wisdom Lodge since they had opened at 10:00 a.m. At eight dollars per person, that wasn't bad for the first two hours of the season. Plus the village was open until 4:00 p.m., and there could still be a significantly sized afternoon crowd.

Mokwa told Joshua that his grandfather also opened up for school groups throughout May, prior to opening for the tourists in June, which brought extra money in.

And Gentle Eagle always made lots of money for the items sold in the Trading Post itself. In fact, it was the Trading Post that brought in most of the money for the village. If only one birchbark canoe sold, that made enough to pay expenses for an entire month. It certainly helped that costs were low. Interns made up the bulk of the workforce, and as today proved, volunteers were invaluable as well.

With so much reliance on free labor, a certain amount of freedom characterized the working conditions at the village. Mokwa and the other volunteers were allowed to teach whatever they wanted. There was no defined curriculum. If one day Mokwa wanted to skip the Wisdom Lodge, for example, he could do so and just spend more time teaching at the Skills Camp. And he was able to cater his teachings to the interests of each tourist. If he sensed boredom from a tourist at one site, he could simply move on to something more interesting. That freedom and spontaneity made working at the village unexpected and fun. One never gave the same tour twice.

It was one of the reasons why Mokwa never had difficulty assembling volunteers whenever Gentle Eagle didn't have enough interns. People loved to volunteer at the village and working with the different people it attracted.

Mokwa told Joshua he'd met Little Deer and Jenny through the village. The reservation was small, and everyone pretty much knew everyone else anyway. But Mokwa hadn't really gotten to know the two until they started volunteering at the village the previous summer. That's when they discovered how much they all had in common.

Now, into the mix, entered Joshua. No one really knew him yet, but because he was Gentle Eagle's grandson, that automatically gave him lots of points. Everyone seemed to revere Gentle Eagle. If he needed them to take a week off from their summer vacation to help out at the village, they gladly obliged. Respect for elders was a strong value on the reservation. Respect for Gentle Eagle far exceeded that expectation.

Mokwa and Joshua sat down for lunch at a picnic table outside the Trading Post. Little Deer and Jenny were already sitting down and comparing stories about how things had gone with the first tourists. With Mokwa and Joshua joining them, the most rewarding part of the whole volunteer experience began—simply hanging out with friends.

"Those two little kids were just adorable," Jenny said, referring to the same two children who had so amused Joshua and Mokwa. "They asked the funniest questions."

"So adorable," Mokwa agreed.

"They couldn't light a fire with the bow drills," Little Deer chimed in, obviously not impressed by cuteness.

"Dude, they were, like, five years old," Mokwa responded. "It's unreasonable to expect young kids to master such a skill."

"They were seven and nine," Jenny corrected.

"All they got was smoke," Little Deer added, continuing with his point.

"I hope you weren't impatient with them," Jenny said, judging her younger brother.

"You don't know me," Little Deer answered.

Joshua just listened. He was always shy around new people and preferred simply to take everything in. Only when he had more information did he like to join in on a conversation with strangers. But the discussion soon turned toward something that interested him.

"Besides, all they wanted to do was talk about Indian names," Little Deer added.

"What do you mean?" Mokwa asked.

"They asked my Ojibwe name at the beginning, and I told them. They got all excited. So I taught them about Ojibwe naming ceremonies. After that, I couldn't get them interested in the bow drill or anything else. And then that little one kept telling me that his Indian name was Otter. And the older one kept badgering me to give him a name."

"What did you name him?" Jenny asked.

"Annoying One," Little Deer replied.

"You didn't!" Mokwa shouted in disbelief.

Little Deer smiled as though he were joking. But his unique grin seemed to mask an underlying sincerity. With his smile, you never quite knew if he were serious or joking. Jenny simply reached over and punched her little brother again.

"Ouch," said Little Deer stoically.

"What is your name in Ojibwe?" Joshua asked Little Deer, trying to get serious.

"*Gidagookoons*," Little Deer responded.

"What does it mean?"

"There is this animal called a deer, and it's little," Little Deer said sarcastically, mocking Joshua.

"Don't make me punch you again," Jenny threatened.

"Yeah, be nice to my new brother," Mokwa said.

Little Deer looked at Joshua as if trying to decipher whether or not he could be trusted. Finally he gave in and explained his name. "The deer is my spirit animal, so Gentle Eagle named me after it."

"Yeah, and like the deer, he's quiet and observes everything," Mokwa said.

"And he doesn't trust anyone," Jenny jumped in, sounding aggravated.

"I trust Mokwa," Little Deer said. "And Gentle Eagle," he quickly added.

"Oh thanks, little brother, for not including your number-one sister."

"You're my only sister."

"I think he gave you the name because you're a vegetarian," Mokwa said.

"You're a vegetarian?" Joshua asked.

Little Deer simply shrugged.

"What about you, Mokwa?" Joshua asked, only then realizing he didn't know what Mokwa's name meant.

"My full name means Angry Bear," Mokwa informed him. "But most people just shorten it to Bear or Mokwa."

It was an odd name, Joshua thought. It didn't seem to fit the Mokwa he had been getting to know. Mokwa seemed friendly and outgoing—nothing like a bear. "What does it mean?" he finally decided to ask.

"So there is this animal called a bear, and it is big and angry," Little Deer interrupted, mocking Joshua once again.

"Little Deer, I'm warning you," Jenny said.

"It means that bravery and confidence are my strongest suits, I suppose. I draw power from the bear."

"You might as well tell him the real reason," Little Deer said. "I don't mind."

Joshua thought that was a curious remark. Was Mokwa hiding something from him? Joshua decided to put that thought aside. He was intrigued by these Indian names. For white people, names had no meaning. They certainly didn't reflect one's nature. Parents just chose them if they thought they sounded good. Although, Joshua thought, sometimes a child was given a name in honor of another relative, like a grandfather. But that didn't reflect a person's identity. If anything, it subsumed one's identity under someone else's name.

"So your name is given to you by an elder?" Joshua asked.

"Well, yes," Mokwa said.

Jenny jumped in. "Parents will often approach an elder and ask them to be their child's 'name-giver,'" she informed Joshua. "Such an elder might take many days, weeks, or even months trying to find the best name. He might pray for a name, or even get one from his or her dreams."

"Oh," said Joshua, acting uninterested when Jenny started talking. "So how do I get a name?"

"You're in luck," Mokwa said. "Gentle Eagle can give you a naming ceremony."

"Yeah," said Jenny. "No one is more qualified than he is. He is an elder and part of the Midewin."

There was that word again associated with his grandfather— *Midewin*. Joshua had to know what it meant.

"What is a—"

"Hey, Joshua!" Mokwa interrupted, as if purposely changing the subject. It was the second time Mokwa had done that when the *Midewin* came up in conversation, Joshua noted.

"You are in for a real treat tonight," Mokwa continued. "We've got a powwow on the Rez tonight. You can't miss it!"

"But I don't know how to dance," Joshua said, concerned that he hadn't yet learned enough from Mokwa.

"Relax, I'm performing. You get to sit and observe. It's a good time."

Joshua decided that watching Mokwa dance was more than worth it, even if he didn't like the powwow itself.

"Here is the Old Man finally," Mokwa said as Gentle Eagle walked out of the Trading Post. "We saved the best spot for you." He pointed to the ground.

"Ha, but I bet you didn't save me any food," Gentle Eagle teased in response.

"Of course I saved you some food," Mokwa said. "We've still got some of the rancid sandwiches that no one else wanted."

"Rancid, my favorite," Gentle Eagle said, going along with the joke.

As Joshua listened, he couldn't ignore the fact that something was going on. Mokwa was very friendly and open, but he was keeping things from him. Mokwa didn't want to talk about the Midewin, and he didn't want to talk about how he got his name. It just didn't make sense. Joshua was determined to learn the truth, even if he had to be patient a little while longer.

FIFTEEN

JOSHUA WAS excited to see his first powwow. It wasn't a "real powwow," Mokwa informed him earlier that day. Rather, it was just a sample exhibition for the casino tourists. Ojibwe powwow exhibition dancing was performed every week in the evening on the reservation, at the campground near the casino, the area where Joshua had jogged earlier that morning. It attracted many tourists from both the campgrounds and from the casino.

So the reservation put on "a powwow without all of the formalities," as Mokwa described it. It would at least give Joshua exposure to some of the different dance styles. He had only been on the reservation for a few days, but already he felt drawn to this alien culture to which he belonged. It was strange and exotic, and yet weirdly familiar at the same time. He took to it immediately.

Hearing about Pukawiss only strengthened his determination to learn everything he could about being an Indian. This was the one place he knew he fit in—where God and the manitous acknowledged and even celebrated him. Joshua never felt that in the Christian faith.

While Joshua never quite took to Christianity, with such a devout mother, he pretended to. He went through the motions, but he didn't embrace it. He didn't fit into it anywhere. Hearing his mother's hate-filled antigay sermons didn't exactly help. Those only deepened the chasm between him and the church. His mother's words became the church's words in Joshua's mind, and he wanted nothing to do with it.

And now he had something better. Now Joshua knew that God did in fact have a place for him. The Ojibwe God did, at least. Mokwa had informed him that God was called Gitchee Manitou. Though often translated as God, Mokwa told him it meant "the Great Mystery." Mostly, people on the reservation simply used the word "Creator" when talking of God. Joshua liked that. There was no dogma attached to it. It was simple and straightforward.

Joshua also wanted to experience this exhibition powwow because it would give him more insight into Pukawiss. After all, according to Mokwa, Pukawiss was the legendary inventor of the powwow.

Of course, Joshua knew there was a more worldly reason he was so excited about the powwow. Mokwa would be dancing. The chance to see Mokwa all decked out in his dance costume was enough to get Joshua out of the house. *Regalia*, Joshua immediately corrected himself. Mokwa had told him never to refer to powwow attire as a costume. The tourists made that mistake all the time.

Joshua arrived quickly at the campground, as it was only a minute from Gentle Eagle's house. He could hear crowds of excited tourists as he approached. When he arrived, he sat down on the grass and awkwardly awaited the beginning of the powwow. About forty people were gathered around the area, some standing, some seated on lawn chairs. Most were obviously tourists.

Some Ojibwe showed up as well, but Mokwa had told him that most were so used to these weekly powwows that they often stayed at home. "They take them for granted," Mokwa had told him. As Joshua looked around, he realized some of the people he assumed to be white tourists could easily be Indians. Mokwa had told him that many of the Indians on the reservation were not full-blooded, just like Joshua.

Joshua immediately took notice when Mokwa arrived at the campground. Mokwa was fortunate because he lived close enough to the campground that he could dress in his regalia at home and simply walk to the powwow. That pretty much applied to everyone living on the reservation, though, Joshua realized. Mokwa noticed Joshua instantly and walked over to him with a brilliant smile on his face.

"Pukawiss! You came to see me!"

Joshua blushed. He had already gotten over his defensiveness over that name. As long as no one took it to mean he was gay, Joshua was fine with it. And the fact that the name was given to him by Mokwa only made it all the more acceptable.

"How could I not come out and support my b...." Joshua paused for a second. "My brother," he said, finishing the sentence. He had almost said "boyfriend." Joshua knew he had to be more careful. He was letting his defenses down.

"I'm honored!" Mokwa said. "Hey, look, it's Jenny and Little Deer!"

"You didn't think I'd miss this?" Jenny accused as she approached with her brother.

"You always miss this," Mokwa said.

"Yeah, but now we got Joshua to watch as well."

"What?" Joshua said, confused.

"You didn't think you were going to just sit here?" Jenny said.

"Yeah, that's what I thought, actually," Joshua mumbled.

"No, this is participatory," Mokwa said to Joshua. "All the tourists will be invited to dance at one point. You'll look dumb if you just sit there. Didn't I tell you this?"

"No," Joshua said scornfully.

"Just remember the basic steps I taught you yesterday," Mokwa reminded him. "You'll do fine. No one expects anything from the observers anyway."

"If I have to dance, you have to dance," Little Deer said to Joshua.

"Wow, are you actually being encouraging?" Jenny said to Little Deer.

Little Deer simply shrugged.

"Dancers, please take your places," the emcee's voice commanded from two large speakers that had been set up for the event.

"Gotta run," Mokwa said as he ran off to a giant circle formed by logs lying on the ground.

The crowd quieted down as the emcee began to speak. Joshua noticed that a few tourists were still talking. The event felt very informal, which seemed to invite small talk among the tourists.

"Boozhoo and welcome to everyone visiting the reservation this week," the emcee said to the audience. "Nothing in life is free, so the saying goes. But tonight is free." After a brief pause, he continued. "Tonight we freely share with you a little taste of our culture. Should your appetite be whetted, please ask one of us about any upcoming larger powwows, and we'll be glad to tell you."

The emcee had a very clear, calm, and polite demeanor. The tourists immediately warmed up to him, and so did Joshua.

"Tonight we'd like to show you a sampling of a few traditional dances," the emcee continued. "You will learn about the Grass Dance, the Fancy Shawl Dance, and maybe I could even find a Fancy Dancer or two willing to show off for you." The emcee looked over to Mokwa. Mokwa nodded back with a smile.

The audience chuckled a bit, enjoying the exchange and accompanying relaxed atmosphere.

"But first, let's introduce you to all of our dancers in a Grand Entry." Four men sitting around a central drum immediately started striking the large drum, creating a steady beat. As they did so, the dancers lined up according to age and began to march out into the arena.

Joshua immediately noticed that they were all doing the two-step technique Mokwa had taught him. The point of the procession, as far as Joshua could tell, was to show off the beautiful regalia of the dancers. It was extremely colorful and impressive, especially for tourists who had never seen anything like it before.

"Feel free to take pictures," the emcee announced, sensing that the visitors were holding back. Immediately flashes started to go off as the tourists reached for their cameras and took shots. "We love all you shutterbugs," the emcee teased.

"I hate pictures," Little Deer said quietly to Jenny and Joshua as the procession continued.

"You hate everything," Jenny whispered back.

"Why do you hate pictures?" Joshua asked Little Deer, hoping to start up a conversation.

Little Deer simply shrugged in response.

Joshua wanted to get to know Little Deer better, but Little Deer wasn't making that easy. He seemed so untrusting. Joshua decided that if Mokwa liked Little Deer, he must be worth getting to know. But Joshua couldn't figure Little Deer out. He said very little, and when he did say something to invite conversation, he just as quickly got quiet again. Perhaps the name "Deer" fit him perfectly after all, Joshua realized. He was shy and suspicious.

Joshua's thoughts were interrupted by the emcee. The Grand Entry was apparently over, and the emcee introduced the next part of the evening.

"In a moment," the emcee said, "you're going to see a sampling of many different types of powwow dances." The audience listened intently. "But first you all need to see for yourself what it's like to powwow dance." Talking and laughter broke out in the audience as the tourists realized what was about to happen.

"And besides, you are our guests. So it wouldn't be fair for us to have all of the fun." The emcee then motioned for Mokwa and two other young dancers to enter the arena and encourage the audience to stand up, join the circle, and dance.

"It doesn't matter whether you know how to dance or not. Just join us and have some fun," the emcee encouraged.

Mokwa had obviously done this before. He walked up to people in the audience in a very gentle and welcoming way. He coaxed them with smiles and motions with his hands. Some people turned him down, but they no doubt felt guilty about it. *Who could turn down Mokwa?* Joshua thought.

After only a few moments, about twenty of the tourists stood in the arena circle with Mokwa and the other Indian dancers. As the drummers began their repetitious and synchronized thumping, Mokwa led the visitors in a two-step dance around the arena. Mokwa still tried to coax audience members to join in, even as he led the procession.

Joshua had stayed seated up until that point, but now he noticed Mokwa staring at him. Joshua knew there was no way out, and he wanted to do this on his own terms. So he stood up and darted over to the arena circle, motioning for Little Deer and Jenny to join him. They obediently followed, but Little Deer did not look happy. Mokwa was obviously pleased that Joshua had joined in on the fun as he continued his dance around the arena.

The whole dance was very informal. Most of the audience members didn't know what they were doing, so no one expected very much. One could see tourists in the circle looking over to Mokwa, desperately trying to imitate him. But most looked awkward and uninitiated.

Joshua, however, looked like a pro as he slowly danced his way up to Mokwa.

"You're really good at this," a pretty-looking Indian girl said, obviously noticing Joshua as he passed her on his way to Mokwa.

Joshua was caught off guard. He hadn't noticed he had an admirer.

"Uh, thanks," he replied awkwardly.

"I haven't seen you here before. Are you camping here?" the girl said.

"No," said Joshua. "I'm visiting my grandfather. He lives here."

"Oh, who is your grandpa?"

"His name is Gentle Eagle."

The girl's face lit up in recognition. "Oh wow," she said. "He's really cool."

"Thanks," Joshua said, wishing the girl would go away. He sped up his pace a bit, hoping the girl would get the clue without his having to more directly hurt her feelings. But as he did so, Joshua noticed a fierce-looking Ojibwe boy, about Mokwa's age, gazing at him angrily from the crowd. He was obviously displeased with Joshua, and for a moment Joshua worried that he had violated some sort of etiquette in rejecting this girl during a dance. Then Joshua realized the teen probably saw Joshua as competition. After all, any straight boy would have found the girl quite alluring.

As Joshua got closer to Mokwa, he continued to scan the crowd. There were still many tourists who had decided not to join in the dancing. Joshua noticed one man in particular who seemed to be closely observing the proceedings—but in a different way from the other tourists. Most people watching the powwow wore shorts and a T-shirt, which was appropriate dress for tourists outside on such a hot day. "White man's costume," Little Deer liked to call it.

But this odd man wore a white dress shirt with a black tie that seemed to uncomfortably strangle his neck. Joshua thought the man looked kind of like the pastor in the church his parents made him attend back in Eagle River. The man seemed so out of place on the reservation.

Most of the people there were either tourists from the casino or campers staying on the campgrounds. Which category did this man fall into? Neither, Joshua decided. The pastor was observing the dancers, but not in the same way as the tourists. The tourists were relaxed and having fun, enjoying the music and the dancing. The pastor seemed unnerved, like he wanted it to stop but knew he could do nothing about it. Joshua wondered why the strange man was there.

He put the man out of his mind as he noticed Little Deer and Jenny catching up with him from behind.

"Are you sure you haven't danced before?" Jenny asked Joshua, obviously impressed with his pace and technique.

"Who is that man?" Joshua asked Little Deer, ignoring Jenny's question.

"An asshole," Little Deer replied.

"That's Pastor Martin," Jenny said, and for once she didn't chastise her brother for being impolite.

"What is a pastor doing at a powwow?" Joshua asked.

"What else is there to do on the Rez?" Little Deer asked.

"You mean he lives here?"

Little Deer shrugged and pointed to a small Baptist church just beyond the campground, set back a bit into the woods. It was smaller than the church his parents went to back in Eagle River, but Joshua reasoned it could easily have a few hundred congregants. That made it quite big for such a small reservation town.

"Yeah, he lives here," Jenny said as though it were obvious. "He's in charge of the church over there."

"Christians? On the reservation?" Joshua muttered, louder than he had anticipated.

"Shocking," Little Deer said a bit sarcastically.

"The French were the first European explorers to encounter the Ojibwe people," Jenny said, finishing his brother's point. "So, Ojibwe and Catholics kind of go way back. And Protestants followed soon thereafter."

"Did you think all Indians followed the traditional ways?" Little Deer asked. It sounded more like a judgment than a question.

"No," Joshua responded defensively. "My father is a Baptist." Joshua thought for a moment as he made a connection. *This must be where he got it from.*

"You mean you're not a Christian?" Jenny asked.

"Let's just say I gave it up for Lent," Joshua responded.

Jenny and Little Deer looked at him as though he had just said something heretical. Joshua tensed up. He didn't mean to be offensive. *What if Little Deer and Jenny are Christians?*

Suddenly, Little Deer burst out into laughter. His dancing pace slowed, and he stumbled and struggled to maintain his balance. Jenny grabbed him by the arm to keep him from falling over, but she was also laughing at Joshua's comment. The tourists looked over to the three to see what was so funny. The more Little Deer tried to contain himself, the harder he laughed. Finally, Jenny let go of him, and he fell to the ground.

"Ouch," he said with laughter still pouring from his mouth.

Joshua stopped dancing and helped Jenny escort Little Deer back to where they had been sitting before the dancing started. Joshua relaxed and even smiled as he started to catch Little Deer's uncontrolled laughter. Beyond that, he was delighted that he finally seemed to have broken through Little Deer's suspicious nature.

"I think we can be friends," Little Deer said as he put his hand out for Joshua.

Joshua enthusiastically grabbed and shook Little Deer's hand. "*Niwiijiwaaganag,*" he said, recalling the word for friends Mokwa had taught him. It was the first time he pronounced an Ojibwe word perfectly the first time.

"Baptists don't do Lent," Jenny finally corrected.

"Shut up," Little Deer said to his sister. "It was funny."

After the "tourist dance," as Little Deer called it, the emcee had everyone sit down and the exhibition dancing began. The tourists were more focused and attentive after having danced themselves. As the night progressed, the emcee introduced various performances and dance styles to the audience.

Joshua took special interest when the emcee announced the "Hoop Dance," because he informed the audience that it had been invented by the legendary Pukawiss. The dance itself involved a man juggling wooden hoops, increasingly taking on more and more hoops as the dance continued.

Joshua watched the Hoop Dancer, transfixed, as the dancer picked up the wooden hoops lying around the circle with his feet—adding one hoop after another to his acrobatic routine. At one point, the whirling dancer held ten interlocking loops that he shaped like wings while dancing. At the end of his performance, he jumped through all the hoops like a jump rope.

As the Hoop Dancer performed this miraculous stunt, the emcee explained its meaning to the audience. He said that the hoops symbolized the various struggles in life that everyone takes on, and how those problems had a habit of multiplying. Eventually, one has to learn to rely on one's own resources to successfully juggle all the hoops. Once you've mastered that, you handle your problems with grace.

Finally, the emcee introduced the dance for which Joshua had been waiting the entire evening. It was time for the Fancy Dance. This was the dance that Mokwa was particularly skilled at. And Joshua couldn't wait to see him perform it. Joshua looked over to Jenny and saw her gawking at Mokwa as she waited for him to begin. It disgusted Joshua that she so visually displayed her objectification of Mokwa. It was demeaning.

As the drummers beat the central drum, the singers joined in with their chants. Joshua immediately fixated on Mokwa as he entered the arena in perfect step with the beat. Joshua and Jenny now gawked in unison.

"*Yo, ah, aye, yo ah, aye,*" the singers chanted in synchrony with the drumming. "*Aha yay, aya aye.*"

As they drummed and chanted, Mokwa matched their rhythm. When they sped up, he sped up; when they slowed down, he slowed down. When they varied the beat, Mokwa always had a crowd-pleasing spin to perform. It was a sight to behold. Joshua could barely even recognize the two-step pattern anymore in the midst of Mokwa's seamless free-form style.

Joshua realized he had a lot to learn if he wanted to be a dancer like Mokwa. But that didn't matter right now. Joshua simply gazed at Mokwa, hypnotized by the chanting, the drumming, the colorful regalia, and by Mokwa's mastery of the Fancy Dance. Powwow dancing was truly a gift of the gods, Joshua realized—a gift of Pukawiss.

Sitting next to Joshua, however, was a constant reminder that he had competition. Joshua felt foolish when he imagined that Mokwa would like him more than Jenny. Jenny was his girlfriend, and Mokwa was clearly straight. But still, such thoughts were easily suppressed when combined with the smitten heart of a fantasizing adolescent. Even as reality kept telling Joshua to give it up, he still entertained the notion that Mokwa secretly wanted him and not Jenny.

Just then Mokwa did a triple pirouette in perfect sync to a completely unanticipated three-drum pounding. The audience erupted in applause. Jenny stood up and cheered for Mokwa.

"So juvenile," Joshua muttered, reacting to Jenny's childish display of affection. Joshua decided he'd strike up a conversation with Jenny in order to distract her from watching Mokwa and further cheering him on.

"So how did Mokwa get his name?" Joshua whispered to Jenny.

She seemed a bit surprised by his question. It was really the first time Joshua had talked to her. "I mean, how did he really get his name?" he repeated. Mokwa himself clearly hadn't wanted to talk about it earlier when it had come up at the village.

"Well, I suppose I can tell you," Jenny whispered back, after seeing Little Deer nod his consent. "A few years ago, Little Deer was getting picked on by some bullies on the reservation, right here at the campground."

Joshua was surprised to hear that. *How does Little Deer figure into the origin of Mokwa's name?*

"There were about three of them ganging up on Little Deer," Jenny continued. "They were calling him all kinds of names and pushing him around."

"Just some stupid douche bags," Little Deer said, acting like it was no big deal.

"It was a big deal. It drives me crazy thinking about it. I showed up and saw them picking on my brother, and I just wanted to...." She suddenly paused. "It infuriates me how cruel people can be. We are all a gift from the Creator. Hurting others denies that gift," Jenny explained as she diverged from Mokwa's origin story.

"Yeah," Little Deer said in agreement. "I'm a damn gift."

"But how did Mokwa get his name?" Joshua interrupted, trying to get Jenny back to the main point.

"Oh yeah, right. Well, so, just as I was about to run after the bullies and do God knows what, I noticed Mokwa come up from behind them. Well, Mokwa just went all apeshit on them, even knocking one of them to the ground with one blow. By the time he was done with them, no one ever dared pick on Little Deer again."

"You said apeshit," Little Deer said, snickering.

"Shut up. Anyway, so that's how he got his name. Yeah, Mokwa is all nice and friendly, and everyone loves that about him, but if someone close to him is threatened, he is like an angry bear protecting his cub."

"I'm his brother, not a cub," Little Deer corrected.

"Whatever," Jenny said. "Anyway, that's when I really took notice of Mokwa for the first time. That won me over. But we didn't start dating till much later, after I started working at the village."

Joshua was amazed by the story. He recalled how angry Mokwa seemed to get earlier when they had an argument about Pukawiss and gays. Joshua had never seen anyone defend gay people before. He was used to his mother's vitriol instead. Mokwa was a true champion in Joshua's eyes.

"That's awesome," Joshua said. "Way to go apeshit on those kids."

"Kids?" Jenny said. "They weren't kids. They were all eighteen and over. Mokwa was only fourteen at the time."

"Definitely has bear power in him," Little Deer said.

Joshua suddenly noticed the older boy who had been staring at him earlier while he was dancing. The boy had an angry scowl on his face, and he was heading straight for Joshua. He gazed directly into Joshua's eyes as he approached. Joshua had no doubt he had done something wrong. *But what?*

"You think you can just come here and take my girlfriend?" the boy said angrily.

"Um" was all Joshua could mutter in response.

Little Deer immediately stood up next to Joshua, signaling to the older boy that if he picked a fight, it would be with both of them.

"I asked you a question, Apple!" the boy said angrily, demanding an answer to his question.

"I don't know what you mean," Joshua finally responded innocently, his voice cracking.

"You can dance like us all you want, Apple, but you'll never be one of us." Then he walked off as quickly as he had approached.

"So, what did you think of your first powwow?" Mokwa said to Joshua when he returned from the dance circle.

Joshua was caught off guard. He hadn't seen Mokwa approach. He'd been so engrossed with the angry intruder that he hadn't even realized the powwow had ended. Joshua tried to put the boy out of his mind. Mokwa was present now, and that's all that mattered.

"You were...." Joshua caught himself and instead offered, "It was amazing."

"Come on, I'll walk you home," Mokwa said.

As Joshua walked home with Mokwa, it was the perfect end to the perfect day. Jenny and Little Deer went the other way, and Mokwa was all his. And Joshua had experienced his first powwow. Or, at least, the first powwow he was old enough to really appreciate. But the thought of that angry boy haunted him a bit. It was obvious he was mad at Joshua for being with his girlfriend. That Joshua could understand. It was a simple misunderstanding. But he'd called Joshua an apple. *What did that mean?*

"The emcee was great too," Joshua said to Mokwa, trying to regain his focus.

"My uncle will be pleased to hear that," Mokwa replied.

SIXTEEN

As JOSHUA arrived at home, Gentle Eagle was repairing a birchbark basket on the couch. He continued to work as though he hadn't noticed Joshua walk in.

"You're sitting on my bed," Joshua teased, trying to get his grandfather's attention. Joshua liked that Gentle Eagle was so easygoing and that he could joke with him. He didn't really have that kind of relationship with his father, or with any adults for that matter.

"Actually, it is you who sleeps on my workbench," Gentle Eagle joked back.

Joshua smiled and sat down next to Gentle Eagle.

"I trust you enjoyed yourself tonight?" Gentle Eagle asked.

"It was amazing," Joshua said as his eyes lit up.

"You seem to be fitting in quite well on the Rez."

Joshua felt so too, but then he recalled the incident with the older boy at the powwow. He thought for a moment that maybe he shouldn't bring it up with his grandfather. But then he realized he didn't have to keep secrets from him. Joshua could tell that Gentle Eagle genuinely cared for him, and maybe he could help. So Joshua finally decided to tell him what had happened. It would be the first time he had ever talked to an adult about his problems.

"Grandfather, at the dance an older boy approached me. He was really mad."

"Oh," said Gentle Eagle. "What was he mad about?"

"Well, there was this girl—"

"Oh, you already have girl problems," Gentle Eagle joked.

"Well, no, I mean, yes, I guess. I mean, she just started dancing with me, and—"

"And he saw you as a threat." Gentle Eagle finished the sentence, perfectly understanding the situation.

"Yeah, but there's more."

"Go on."

"He called me an apple. Did I misunderstand him? Is that some kind of Ojibwe word?"

Gentle Eagle sighed and looked a bit concerned. It seemed like he was going to change the subject, but then he put his arm around Joshua.

"No, it is definitely not an Ojibwe word, my grandson."

"Then what did he mean by it?"

"Did this boy look to be about Mokwa's age, by any chance?"

"Yes!" Joshua said, surprised. "Do you know him?"

"His name is Black Crow, and everyone knows him. He called you an apple, as in red on the outside and white on the inside."

"What?"

"It's his way of saying that you are not a real Indian, my grandson."

"Oh," Joshua responded, trying to suppress the sting. But he was distressed, and Gentle Eagle could obviously tell.

"Not everyone here is like Black Crow," Gentle Eagle said. "You have some great friends here on the Rez, my grandson. And you belong here with them. Don't let anyone tell you otherwise."

Joshua smiled as he reflected on Mokwa and Little Deer, and even Jenny. But he was still distressed. He had never really felt like an Indian before, since his family had suppressed that part of his heritage. But now, just as he was beginning to learn about his culture and embrace his identity, this Black Crow had to take it all away from him. Joshua felt somehow inadequate, even fake. He didn't like feeling like an outsider. He had already been thrown out like a piece of garbage by his mother, after having been abandoned by his father. Now he felt rejected by his new family too. He was an outcast in both words. Joshua decided now wasn't the time to dump all this on his grandfather.

"Thanks," was all he said in response to Gentle Eagle. "If it's okay, I'd like to go to bed now."

Gentle Eagle looked like he was going to say something, but then he paused.

"Of course," he finally responded as he stood up to head to his bedroom. "It's getting late."

JOSHUA DREAMED he was standing in the middle of a large circle in a giant grass arena. Lawn chairs outlined the circle and were filled with people. They were spectators, Joshua realized. But what were they watching? Joshua heard drums beating and chanting in the background. Then he realized he was at a powwow. But this was nothing like the powwow he had just witnessed in real life. It was much larger. There were many hundreds of people in the audience observing. And they weren't watching Mokwa; they were watching him.

Joshua suddenly noticed another dancer in the arena, farther down from him. He was dancing spectacularly to the amazement of the crowds. Joshua only caught a glimpse of this other dancer as he was concentrating on his own performance. Joshua was dancing for the crowds, and he was good at it. His dance flowed effortlessly, almost as though he was channeling Mokwa. He flawlessly executed Mokwa's moves. Then the drums suddenly stopped beating as Joshua performed his own signature maneuver. He looked up to the thunderous applause of hundreds of spectators. It felt great. Joshua awoke feeling more alive than ever. Usually he needed to take his morning jog before feeling so vibrant, but this dream totally revitalized him. It also motivated him. He was determined after that dream to learn how to dance like Mokwa.

Joshua mostly tried to ignore his dreams, as they were often nonsensical—or sometimes disturbing, especially when it was hot, Joshua reflected. But it was getting increasingly difficult for him to do so. His dreams seemed to counter his disinterest in them by putting elements in that forced him to pay attention.

Joshua got off the couch and tugged at his boxers, which were sticking to him. *This heat is crazy,* Joshua thought. *I so need a fan.* He didn't even bother to look at the clock. He just assumed it was 5:00 a.m. and time for his morning jog. Thoughts from his dream stayed with him as he dressed and ran out the door. He couldn't get them out of his head, nor did he want to. He had never felt so alive. The chants were spellbinding.

Joshua picked up his pace and made his way to his favorite jogging path along the lakeshore. As always, the lake was lined with campers, many of whom had attended the previous night's powwow. Joshua realized that no one was up. It was typical for him to be mostly alone when he ran in the morning, but usually at least a few people were stirring by then. Mokwa ran early as well, Joshua recalled.

Only then did he realize that it was a bit darker than normal. The sun hadn't even risen above the forests on the horizon along the other side of the lake. Joshua didn't care. He wasn't tired at all, and he decided to continue with his jog. But when he arrived at the lake, he had to stop and gaze at the sunrise as it emerged from the trees. It was so brilliant and radiant that he couldn't turn away.

As he gazed at the warm and vibrant energy of the sun, he heard the chanting again from his dreams. The music beckoned him, and Joshua responded accordingly. He started to dance. He placed his right foot forward and double-tapped to the chants in his head, just like Mokwa had taught him. He quickly pulled his second leg forward and repeated the pattern. But this dance was not to be anything as formal and simple as the grand entry double-step dance. Joshua felt something much greater stirring. He let the chanting possess him, allowing his body to move naturally to the rhythm. The sun was now halfway up above the horizon, and the beams of light created a beautiful silhouette as he twisted and turned to the chanting and drumming in his head. As the sun disc finally emerged completely for the day, the drums in Joshua's head suddenly stopped beating. And so did Joshua, perfectly on cue.

But Joshua knew his dance needed something more. He didn't remember exactly what he'd done to get so much applause in his dream, but he knew he had executed something really amazing at the very end of the dance. He didn't know what it was, but he was going to recall it. Instead of running, Joshua realized, he was going to come down to this lake every morning and Fancy Dance until he got it right—until it was perfect. No one, Joshua thought, would ever again question whether or not he was a real Indian.

LATER IN the day, after a group of tourists had left the Wisdom Lodge, Mokwa had a surprise in store for Joshua.

"Joshua, I have to go," he explained. "I have to pick up some supplies for Gentle Eagle."

"Who will staff this site?" Joshua asked, sounding concerned.

"You are ready to do it," Mokwa responded confidently.

"Are you joking?" Joshua barked as his heart beat faster.

"Pukawiss, my brother, you can do this."

"What if I forget the meaning of a word?" Joshua said, panicking.

"Then make something up," Mokwa advised. "Who will know?"

"Well, what if I forget a myth I'm telling halfway through?" Joshua added, desperately trying to find another excuse.

"Calm down. You won't forget anything," Mokwa said, "and it doesn't have to be exact. Just know the main point."

"What if I forget the main point?"

"Oh my God, Joshua! I love you, bro, gotta go." Mokwa ran off down the trail. He shouted back to Joshua, "You'll do fine!"

Joshua sat down on a stump in front of the Wisdom Lodge, reviewing relevant Ojibwe words he could use for the tourists. Boozhoo, of course, was standard. *Migwetch*, he thought as his mind searched for other words. "Yeah, that's a classic," he murmured. *Maybe some animal names too. Everyone likes animals.*

Joshua also had to figure out which story to tell. Would he remember all the elements to the story he chose? After thinking about it for a bit, Joshua decided he would simply repeat the story of Nanaboozhoo and the Flood that Mokwa had told.

As he mentally reviewed the story, he heard a group of tourists coming up the trail. He immediately tensed up. Joshua stood up in front of the Wisdom Lodge and awaited their arrival. *You can do this*, Joshua told himself. *Don't panic.*

There were three tourists, all adults, Joshua noted. *Why couldn't they be kids? I don't know how to handle adults.*

"Boozhoo!" Joshua said to the visitors as they entered the area. He had practically shouted it. *Keep it down a bit,* he chided himself. Sweat began to accumulate on his forehead.

"*Boo* what?" the first of the three visitors said back.

"Oh, it means hello," Joshua informed them.

"So why didn't you just say hello," the tourist said rudely.

Joshua wasn't expecting that. Mokwa had told him this would be easy. All the tourists he had seen so far went out of their way to be nice and open-minded. But these guys seemed different. Joshua sensed something was off about them right away. *Whatever*, Joshua thought. *So I won't use any Ojibwe words.* He decided simply to continue.

"My name is Joshua, and I'll be your guide today."

"You mean our scout?" the man said jokingly as he made the quotation mark symbol with two of his fingers. The other two with him laughed.

"Sure, whatever," Joshua responded, not knowing what to make of his comment. He brushed it off and continued.

"I'm going to teach you some Ojibwe myths today," Joshua told them.

"So what kind of Indian name is Joshua anyway?" the third man asked.

"Well, it's my English name," Joshua responded.

"Why don't you have an Indian name?" the man challenged. "Ain't you a real Indian?"

Joshua paused for a moment and then tried to continue.

"Anyway, I want to tell you the story of Nanaboozhoo," he said, hoping his visitors would be quiet.

"We don't want to learn about any Nanny Boohoo," the men said irreverently. "We're here for the weapons."

"Yeah," the second man agreed. "Where do you keep the bows and arrows and hatchets?"

"Um, over there down that trail," Joshua informed them before realizing what he had just done.

Oh no, Joshua thought, *That's Little Deer's site. These guys will eat Little Deer up for lunch.*

"Well, you've been a great scout," the first man said, pausing for a moment before sarcastically emphasizing, "Joshua."

The men started to walk toward the trail to the Skills Camp. Suddenly they stopped, as if realizing they had forgotten something. The third man reached into his backpack and pulled out a can of beer. He handed one to each of the other two men but he fumbled and dropped one on the trail.

Joshua couldn't believe it. Alcohol was not permitted at the village. There was a sign at the entrance that clearly said so. His grandfather even told every tourist the rule when they purchased their tickets at the Trading Post. They had probably just snuck in, he determined.

What do I do now? Joshua asked himself. Mokwa hadn't prepared him in how to enforce the rules.

"Um, excuse me, guys," Joshua called to the visitors. He ran up to them by the trail. "Hey, sorry to bother you, but there is no drinking here."

The men all laughed.

The first man took a sip of his beer and let out a big sigh. "Mmmm," he said.

His friend jumped in. "Well, thanks for that information, Joshua." Again, the man mockingly emphasized his name.

The men continued up the trail toward Little Deer. Joshua was stunned at their disrespect. It wasn't just that they violated a rule; it was an extraordinarily special rule. Alcohol was a major problem on the reservation. And there was a long history of whites using alcohol to get Indians drunk to get them to sign away their lands. It also affected Joshua very personally, as his father was an alcoholic, though Joshua barely acknowledged it.

Joshua had never felt so small in his life. He had come to have so much pride and joy in his heritage over the past couple of days, and he was so excited to share it. But now he just felt like a coward.

Then he recalled what Mokwa had done to the group of bullies who had picked on Little Deer. Mokwa was Joshua's age at the time, and the bullies were grown adults. Joshua realized that all it took was a show of force. His humiliation transformed into determination. He was not going to let these guys get away with disrespecting himself or his culture. Joshua was resolute. He would summon his own bear power, just like Mokwa had done.

Joshua ran up the trail after the three men. "Hey, hold on a second!" he shouted.

After a moment on the trail, Joshua could see that the three tourists were already at the Skills Camp. They were surrounding Little Deer, who looked very uncomfortable.

"Hey!" Joshua repeated as he entered the site. Little Deer immediately looked relieved.

"Hey, it's our good friend, Joshua," the first man said.

"Hey, Joshua, why are you following us?" the second man added.

"Yeah," the third man said, "that's kind of weird."

Joshua summoned all his strength. He looked the first man right in the eyes, determined to meet his gaze. Then he walked firmly toward him.

"Pukawiss ndishnikaaz!" Joshua shouted to the three men. "Now put the damn beer down, pick up the can you left on the trail, and get the hell out of here!" Joshua screamed louder than he ever thought possible.

Silence befell the surrounding forests, as though an actual bear had just roared. Joshua just stood there, tall and proud.

The three men looked like deer staring at headlights. They clearly had not expected a kid to chew them out like that. One of the three men looked like he was about to respond, when Little Deer preempted him.

"The man said pick up the can!"

Little Deer lifted his bow and pulled an arrow from his quill. After a small fraction of a second, which he used to sight his target, he let an arrow fly. It whooshed into the forest, barely hitting some low-hanging branches. A second later the arrow smacked into the beer can center on, piercing its metal and sticking into the ground beneath it. Beer spurted from it, showering the plants all around.

The three men obediently put their cans away and ran down the trail. The first man picked up the can with the arrow in it, while the other two continued to run. The man watched his friends, as if wondering if he should follow, and then he turned back toward Joshua and Little Deer.

"Here," the man said sheepishly as he handed them the can. He then turned and ran after his friends.

Joshua was elated. It was the first time he had ever encountered bullies before, and he'd successfully challenged them. He'd exhibited true courage for the first time in his life. He'd defended his heritage and his friend, and the bullies had backed down. It was a feeling he would never forget.

Joshua put his arm on Little Deer's shoulder. "That was an amazing shot!" he said.

"You said a bad word," Little Deer replied back.

Joshua laughed. "I hope you don't tell my grandfather."

"If you don't tell him I almost shot those three men," Little Deer replied.

"It's a deal," Joshua said as they shook hands. "Let's get lunch. I think we earned it."

The two walked up the trail to the Trading Post for their lunch break with a newfound respect for each other.

As they approached, Joshua noted an older Indian boy standing by the front door of the Trading Post, as though he were waiting for someone. The boy noticed Joshua and Little Deer approaching, and he turned and gazed right at them. Joshua realized it was Black Crow, the angry boy from the powwow.

"Oh no, this is not happening," Joshua said to Little Deer.

"Should I get my bow?" Little Deer offered.

Joshua couldn't tell if he was serious or not.

"There you are, Apple," Black Crow said in a mocking tone.

"His name is Joshua," Little Deer barked.

Black Crow bellowed at the announcement. "Joshua, eh? You don't even have an Indian name," he teased.

"I do so," Joshua said, feeling insecure.

"You do?" Little Deer whispered.

"Shhhh," Joshua said, quieting Little Deer. He then turned confidently to face Black Crow. "My name is Pukawiss!" he proudly informed him.

Black Crow didn't look impressed. Instead he looked angry. "Naming yourself after a manitou? That's sacrilege!" he shouted.

He approached Joshua as though he were going to hit him. Joshua instinctively covered his face. But the punch never came. Instead Joshua sensed a shadow between himself and Black Crow. He dared to open his eyes and immediately saw what happened. It was Mokwa, back from his chores and standing in front of Joshua like an angry bear.

"I gave him his name!" Mokwa shouted. "Do you have a problem with that?" Joshua saw a cardinal flutter by, obviously disturbed by the fight.

Black Crow seemed humbled but not satisfied. He glared at Joshua with contempt but seemed to respect Mokwa. He turned around and walked away. As he reached his car in the parking lot, he shouted back to Joshua.

"Your friends can give you nice-sounding names, but you're still just an apple, and everyone knows it." He sped off in his car, leaving a loud screech behind. Just as Black Crow's car pulled away, another car pulled in.

"Great," said Little Deer, "more tourists."

"Those aren't tourists," Mokwa said. "It's Pastor Martin."

As Joshua got a good look at the man's face, he recalled seeing Pastor Martin at the powwow the night before. The man had seemed so awkward at the powwow, but he seemed even more out of place at a recreated Ojibwe village. *What does Pastor Martin want here?* Joshua had a bad feeling about this.

SEVENTEEN

"QUICK, COME with me," Mokwa whispered frantically to Joshua and Little Deer, motioning them to follow him into the woods. The three ducked behind some trees, just as Pastor Martin got out of his car and headed toward the Trading Post.

"Why is he here?" Joshua asked, curious at everyone's strange reaction.

"It's Pastor Martin," Little Deer said, unexcitedly.

"He runs the local Baptist church," Mokwa informed Joshua.

"Yeah, I know. Why are we hiding?" Joshua asked.

"He comes around here every once in a while, mostly to talk with Gentle Eagle," Mokwa said.

"He sees Wiigwaas Village as a threat," Little Deer added.

"Threat?" Joshua said.

"Yes," Little Deer said. "This place makes his job more difficult." Little Deer paused for a moment, as though he were thinking about his next words carefully. "You can't convert the devil worshippers if they hang on to false beliefs," he said stoically, but with a slight hint of sarcasm.

"I think you are exaggerating a bit," Mokwa said.

"He thinks I'm going to hell," Little Deer responded.

"Whatever," Mokwa said, wanting to dismiss the argument. It was typical of Mokwa to see the good in everyone, just as it was typical of Little Deer to be suspicious of everyone. Joshua thought the two made an interesting pair.

"So why does he come to talk to Gentle Eagle? Are they friends?" Joshua asked. He thought that if Gentle Eagle was friends with Pastor Martin, then he must be okay.

"Gentle Eagle gets along with everyone," Mokwa responded. "It's kind of in his name."

Jenny arrived from the Moon Lodge and noticed the three boys crouched down whispering to each other behind a small tree.

"Hey, having a party back there?" she shouted.

"Shhhhh," Mokwa chided.

"What's going on?"

"Pastor Martin is in there talking to Gentle Eagle," Mokwa informed Jenny. "And we're trying to figure out why."

"He wants to do an exorcism," Little Deer said.

"That's only Catholics," Jenny said.

"Shut up," Little Deer countered.

"I think he's trying to convert Gentle Eagle," Mokwa said.

"No way, he would never waste his time like that," Jenny said.

"So, why don't we just listen in?" Joshua suggested.

Mokwa, Little Deer, and Jenny stopped talking and stared directly at Joshua.

"Are you saying that we should spy on Gentle Eagle?" Mokwa asked.

"It was just a thought," Joshua said, feeling awkward.

"Let's go," his three friends said in unison as they got up to listen underneath an open window in the Trading Post. Joshua ran after them.

"You know she's right," the three overheard Pastor Martin saying to Gentle Eagle.

"I know she thinks she's right," Gentle Eagle said.

"She is the father of that boy, and her wishes need to be respected," Pastor Martin insisted.

"I am respecting her wishes. I always have," Gentle Eagle said calmly.

"You have him working out here in this, this...." Pastor Martin paused for a moment. "You know what you do here," he finally said accusingly. "You know what the point of this place is."

"I know. I created it. The point is for our people not to be ashamed of where they came from."

"You have impressionable youth working here," Pastor Martin said forcefully.

"I've noticed some adults are as well."

"You are teaching Joshua the old ways."

Joshua finally understood that the two were arguing about him. Mokwa looked at Joshua quizzically as Jenny and Little Deer strained to hear more.

"Joshua is not learning the old ways," Gentle Eagle corrected. "I haven't taught him anything."

"Have you taught him about the Midewin?" Pastor Martin said in an accusatory tone. "Is that what you're doing to Joshua? Fixing the mistake you made with your own son?"

Midewin? There was that mysterious word again, Joshua thought. What did it mean? And why did everyone keep changing the subject whenever he brought it up?

"My son made his own mistakes, and he is still paying for them," Gentle Eagle said.

"You are leading your grandson away from God!" Pastor Martin asserted.

"Pastor, I'm always happy to have a civilized conversation with you. But when you start acting like a savage, then the conversation is over."

"Fine, then may I assume you have no problem with me talking to the boy myself?" Pastor Martin asked.

"I'm sure that can be arranged."

"Without you there?" Pastor Martin asked, challenging Gentle Eagle.

Gentle Eagle paused. "If I'm not present, then I'm afraid you won't have a chance," he said cryptically.

"Fine, then it's agreed. I'll talk with him now."

"Now?" Gentle Eagle said.

"Is that a problem?"

"It's 1:00 p.m.," Gentle Eagle said. "The boy is working."

"Here are eight bucks, then," Pastor Martin said. "Consider me a tourist."

"Oh shit," the three spies whispered, looking at each other frantically. "We've got to get to our posts!" The three ran off while Joshua waited behind, feeling frustrated.

"Wait!" Joshua called to Mokwa.

"Joshua, we've got to go," Mokwa said, obviously avoiding him.

"Quickly, I just want to know what the Midewin are?" Joshua asked as he ran to catch up with Mokwa.

"It's past one o'clock," Mokwa said. "We've got to get to work."

"Mokwa?" Joshua called again. "You are my brother."

Mokwa seemed to realize he couldn't evade the subject any further. He sighed and slowed down, allowing Joshua to catch up with him. Finally, he stopped and put his arm around Joshua's shoulder.

"You are right. I promise I'll tell you everything that you want to know later. It wasn't right for me to keep this from you."

Mokwa started to run away again, this time heading toward the storage shelter at the end of the Village. "You've got the Wisdom Lodge the rest of the afternoon," he called back to Joshua. "I'll see you at closing time."

"Okay, later, then," Joshua said. "And don't forget your promise!" Joshua wasn't sure if Mokwa heard him, but he was determined to make sure Mokwa would tell him everything he had been hiding.

EIGHTEEN

JOSHUA PACED nervously back and forth upon returning to the Wisdom Lodge for the afternoon. He mentally reviewed the troubling conversation he had just overheard between his grandfather and Pastor Martin.

Midewin? What was that mysterious word? Joshua had heard it several times from Mokwa. And now, he heard it from this strange Pastor Martin, who seemed terrified of the word. Mokwa appeared anxious about it as well—or, at least, anxious not to tell Joshua about it. *What could be so frightening about that word?*

He finally calmed down a bit as he recalled that Mokwa had promised to tell him everything later. All he had to do was be patient and make it through the afternoon.

But as Joshua put one troubling thought out of his mind, another surfaced. This pastor knew something about Joshua's father. He had said something about his father making a mistake. *What was the mistake?*

Joshua had a difficult time even imagining his father on the reservation, despite the fact that his father had grown up there. His father had left it at some point, but Joshua was never told when or why. Now he wanted answers.

The mental wrestling abated as Joshua heard leaves rustling on the trail coming up from the Trading Post. He tensed again for a moment, wondering if the three creepy tourists were back for more trouble. But he didn't care. He felt like he could take on anyone right now. Surely he could defend himself against a bunch of drunken bigots.

Then Joshua noticed it was Pastor Martin, and he was approaching fast. *What does he want?* Joshua wondered. First Pastor Martin had confronted Gentle Eagle, and now he was coming to talk to Joshua. And why did his grandfather not come with? Something just wasn't right.

"Boozhoo," Joshua said, greeting the pastor as if nothing was wrong. He certainly didn't want this man to know that he had been spying on him.

Pastor Martin simply smiled and responded, "Boozhoo, Joshua."

"Oh, you know my name?" Joshua said, feigning ignorance.

The man ignored the question for a moment, as he looked around the site. He then gazed at Joshua's Indian clothing.

"I see you are dressed appropriately for the sixteenth century," Pastor Martin said to Joshua. "It's a very authentic costume."

"Regalia," Joshua corrected, a bit perturbed. But he calmed himself. He wanted to find out what this guy was all about.

"Oh, I'm sorry. Of course, regalia," Pastor Martin corrected himself. "We must always remember the important things," he added, sounding a bit sarcastic.

Joshua didn't know what Pastor Martin meant by that, but it gnawed at him.

Just then, Joshua saw Little Deer enter the site from the Skills Camp. He must have seen Pastor Martin. Little Deer was prepared to rescue him, Joshua mused. *It's nice when someone has your back.*

"So what do you think about this place, Joshua?" Pastor Martin asked.

"How do you know my name exactly?" Joshua asked.

"My apologies, of course, you don't know me. I'm Pastor Martin," he said, extending his hand, which Joshua reluctantly shook.

"Yeah, I know you."

"Oh," said Pastor Martin.

"Yeah," said Joshua. "I saw you at the powwow last night. You looked uncomfortable."

"I'm sure you are mistaken, Joshua. I quite enjoy those weekly powwows. They are a good opportunity for me to interact with...." He paused, as if he wanted to be careful about his words. "With my congregants," he finally said.

"You mean your sheep?" Little Deer jumped in. Pastor Martin ignored the insult and offered his hand. "Good to see you again, Little Deer."

Little Deer didn't take his hand. He simply stared at him in the characteristically stoic way he adopted around strangers. Little Deer could stare down a *wendigo*, Joshua thought. The wendigo was a particularly fearsome, almost demonic manitou that haunted the northern forests. It would devour a person alive, if it caught him, and it was very fast, Mokwa had informed Joshua.

Pastor Martin put his hand down, seeing he wasn't going to get anywhere. Little Deer was a distraction anyway. The pastor was there for Joshua.

"I'm a friend of your grandfather's," Pastor Martin said.

"That's funny, because he never mentioned you," Joshua said suspiciously.

"I'm sure there is a lot he hasn't told you."

"Or you," Little Deer said.

Pastor Martin again ignored the insult. "Although I'm mostly interested in what he has taught you, as opposed to what he has left out."

"What do you mean?" Joshua asked.

"It strikes me that working here is a great way to be exposed to all aspects of Ojibwe culture."

"What do you want?" Little Deer said.

"I'm just here to look around," Pastor Martin replied. "I always like to see what Gentle Eagle has done with the place. It's grown quite a bit over the years. Very impressive."

"Yeah, working here is great," Joshua said. "I've made some really good friends."

"Such as Little Deer?" the pastor inquired. It was more of a statement than a question, though.

Joshua put his hand around Little Deer's shoulder as if in solidarity.

"Yes, like Little Deer," Joshua affirmed.

"Well, about this place. It's a good thing that your grandfather is trying to do here. It's nice to preserve the past," Pastor Martin said. "You can't move on unless you know where you came from."

"Well, half of me came from the Europeans," Joshua said. "And the other half came from the Ojibwe. But up till now, I've only been taught about the first half."

"Well, Joshua, what is important about history is that it teaches us how to live in the present. Do you understand?"

Little Deer rolled his eyes.

"Not really," Joshua said, suspecting it was a loaded question.

"The Europeans came over here and encountered people with very different values and lifestyles. And some of those ways were inferior to what the Europeans had." Pastor Martin paused and then continued. "The Europeans gave the Ojibwe pots and guns and writing and, well, even a very different understanding of God."

"They also took some things," Little Deer said.

"Mistakes were made, naturally. Humans are never perfect. But we learned to put aside those differences."

"After you were done taking everything," Little Deer accused.

"I really don't know where all this hostility comes from, Little Deer. I'm simply saying that while it's fun to learn about the past, let's live in the present."

"The present?" Joshua asked, hoping for clarification.

"Don't trust him," Little Deer said.

"Joshua, your little friend is exactly right. I'm not being entirely sincere. I have an agenda. Don't we all? This is all really an invitation. Come by my church sometime, and we'll talk. The church is the present. And the future too. You don't have to believe that. I just want for us to be able to talk to each other."

"Talk? Or preach," Little Deer said.

"I promise I will listen as well," Pastor Martin said, unfazed by the accusation.

"What would we talk about exactly?" Joshua asked.

"Well, perhaps we could talk about your father," he said as he headed for the trail. He stopped and turned to face Joshua again. "And maybe we can talk about the Midewin as well."

Joshua tried to imitate Little Deer's stoic look. "I see from your expression you've heard of them," Pastor Martin said. "Anyway, come by the church any time you want," he called back as he walked down the trail. "Consider it a standing invitation," he shouted before disappearing from their sight.

Joshua realized that he had to give Pastor Martin credit. He knew exactly what would entice Joshua to come to his church. This man, whatever his motives, knew something about Joshua's father. And Joshua was intent on discovering what. But first he had to learn about the Midewin. Joshua eagerly anticipated the end of the day to have that conversation with Mokwa.

NINETEEN

JOSHUA HAD many more tourists come through the Wisdom Lodge after Pastor Martin left, and by the end of the afternoon, he felt more confident about running the site without Mokwa. But nothing could put the incident with Pastor Martin out of his mind. He was both excited and anxious to discuss it with Mokwa. Furthermore, he was as determined as ever to learn about his father, as well as the mysterious Midewin.

At closing time, Joshua walked to the Trading Post and met up with Mokwa, helping him close down the village for the night. Closing down the village was quite involved. They had to walk around to each site and make sure nothing was left out—pelts, baskets, weapons—everything had to be put away in case of rain. Each of the wigwams had to be covered as well. But Mokwa didn't forget his promise to Joshua. He invited him out for pizza to discuss everything that was on his mind. Gentle Eagle wanted to stay late at the village to finish up some projects and happily agreed to let Joshua spend more time with his friends.

Joshua was happy to see that Little Deer would be joining them. He had gotten used to Little Deer's cutting sense of humor and felt more comfortable around him now. He also had a newfound respect for Little Deer after the way he had handled the creepy tourists. Jenny would be coming along with them as well, but Joshua decided he would try to keep his jealousy at bay. He was determined to learn about the Midewin no matter what; his childish adolescent obsessions had to take a backseat.

It was about a twenty-minute drive to the tourist town located just outside the reservation boundaries. Little Deer spent most of the ride bringing Jenny and Mokwa up to speed on the earlier exchange with Pastor Martin.

Joshua noted that the town pretty much had everything the reservation lacked—a bowling alley, strip malls, a wide selection of restaurants, and most importantly to Joshua, a movie theater. But it was the pizza place that got most of the attention from reservation teens.

Joshua tried to put these distractions out of his mind, since he wanted to get down to business. As he sat down at a booth in the pizza place next to Mokwa, Joshua dived right into the mystery Mokwa had promised to discuss with him.

"So, what are the Midewin?" he asked as soon as the waitress finished taking their order.

"Wow," said Jenny. "You don't beat around the bush."

"Yeah, let's at least wait for the food," Little Deer added.

"Mokwa, you promised me," Joshua reminded him in a pathetic tone.

"Oh man, you're good," said Mokwa. "Who could resist those cute green eyes of yours?"

With that unexpected tease, Joshua immediately forgot about the Midewin. Mokwa had the power to completely control Joshua's thoughts and emotions. Joshua wanted to try and just be friends with Mokwa and let him be happy with his girlfriend. But Mokwa didn't make that easy. His flirtations kept toying with Joshua's emotional state. Or at least Joshua interpreted it as flirting. Maybe Mokwa didn't see it that way. Mokwa was straight, after all, Joshua knew. *Or is he bisexual?* Joshua mentally entertained that notion for a few seconds. Only then did he realize that Mokwa had managed to distract him from the Midewin once again. Joshua knew that he had to focus on the subject at hand.

"Your green eyes are kind of cute," Little Deer said.

"Yeah, Joshua, I can hook you up with some nice Ojibwe girls. Kiwi was sure checking you out at the powwow the other night."

Joshua's face turned bright red. "Kiwi?" he said.

"Yeah, Kiwidinok—the hot chick you were dancing with," Mokwa said. "Her name means 'Woman of the Wind.'" As Mokwa said her name, his tone sounded envious, and his eyes fluttered. "But I like to call her *Zaasakokwaan*, or Frybread, because, mmmm, she is irresistible."

Jenny shot Mokwa an irritated glance.

"Sorry, I mean she is an intellectually superior and in no way objectified goddess," Mokwa corrected himself. Jenny nodded, obviously pleased with how well she had trained Mokwa.

"Ha, Pukawiss, you barely know how to dance, and you're already more popular with the ladies than I am," Mokwa teased.

"You just keep that popularity in check," Jenny warned Mokwa, mostly joking.

"Don't worry, Jenny, you know you are my one and only true love," Mokwa assured her. "Well, besides Joshua, of course," he added.

Joshua sighed even as he blushed. "Mokwa, please tell me about the Midewin," he said, desperately trying to get the conversation back on track.

Mokwa looked like he was going to continue with his flirtation, but then he paused. "Okay, fine, I'll tell you—"

Just then, the waitress arrived and placed a large pizza on the table, interrupting their discussion. Mokwa immediately got quiet, as though they were having a top secret conversation. Joshua was annoyed by the intrusion. He just couldn't get a break. *She'll only be a second,* Joshua thought. *Just calm down.*

The waitress put the pizza down and turned to walk away. "Finally," Joshua murmured impatiently.

The waitress turned around suddenly, realizing she had forgotten something. "So, can I get you anything else?" she politely asked.

"No," Joshua barked, clearly sounding annoyed. "That will be all," he added dismissively.

"Oh wait, I forgot your pitcher," the waitress added. "Where is my brain today?"

Joshua threw his head down to the table in frustration. It made a loud thump. "Ouch," he said softly.

"Yeah, even I felt that," Little Deer said.

"Okay, Joshua, I'll tell you about the Midewin," Mokwa said as the waitress finally walked away to get their pitcher of soda.

"Can someone pass me a slice of pizza?" Little Deer said in frustration, as he was out of reach.

Joshua handed a slice of sausage pizza over to Little Deer. "Go on," he said to Mokwa, still listening intently.

"Okay, so the Midewin are—"

"I don't like sausage," Little Deer said sullenly.

"Oh my God, take it!" Joshua said in frustration as he grabbed the entire pizza and moved it over to Little Deer. "This half is all cheese. Have at it." Joshua felt bad for acting like a jerk to Little Deer, but nothing else mattered to him at that moment. He was about to learn the great secret everyone was keeping from him.

"Okay, so the Midewin are—"

"Here you go," the waitress said enthusiastically as she put a pitcher of soda on the table.

"Shoot me now," Joshua said as he slammed his face back on the table.

"Let me know if you need anything else," the waitress offered.

"Okay," Joshua's muffled voiced responded.

As the waitress left, Joshua popped his head back up.

"Well?"

"Okay, so I wasn't supposed to tell you any of this," Mokwa said. "That's why I've been reluctant to talk about it."

"What do you mean?" Joshua asked.

"Gentle Eagle asked me not to say anything. And when he asks you not to do something, you listen. He's an elder, and he's my friend."

"Okay, so why doesn't he want me to know? What are the Midewin exactly?"

"They are sort of a secret society of—" Mokwa paused for a second. "—of medicine men," he finally said. "Their job is to preserve the old ways. They are powerful shamans."

"Why is that a secret?" Joshua asked.

"Well, when the Christians tried to stomp out Ojibwe religion, they saw the Midewin as a threat. Many were persecuted. That sort of forced them underground, so to speak."

"So that's why Pastor Martin brought them up?" Joshua asked.

"Mostly," Little Deer jumped in.

"Yeah," said Mokwa.

"What does any of this have to do with me?" Joshua asked. "Why did Pastor Martin want to know if I heard about them?"

"He is just paranoid," Little Deer said. "If we are telling you about the Midewin, it means to him that we are 'converting' you."

"Yeah," said Jenny. "To Pastor Martin that's like the dark side."

"One less convert to the one true faith," Little Deer said.

"But I still don't know what my father, or my grandfather, has to do with all of this," Joshua said, confused. "It doesn't make sense."

Little Deer looked like he was about to talk, but Mokwa motioned for him to be quiet.

"I told you that I'd tell you about the Midewin," Mokwa said to Joshua. "But you'll have to get the rest from your grandfather."

Joshua understood. He didn't like that he had already forced Mokwa to break his promise. And he had no problem talking directly with his grandfather. He had proven to be very easy to talk with. So with that solved, Joshua was determined to enjoy the rest of the evening.

"Hey, Joshua!" a strikingly beautiful girl said as she walked up to the table where Joshua was sitting. It was Kiwi. She acknowledged Joshua's friends with a quick, almost dismissive nod, then got back to her true target.

"I liked your dancing the other day," she said, beaming.

"Aren't you dating Black Crow?" Jenny stated matter-of-factly, obviously perturbed by Kiwi's flirtation.

"We broke up," she said, barely taking her eyes off of Joshua. "So I'm free to mingle with whomever I want." She sat down next to Joshua, pressing up against him.

"Tell me, has any lucky girl on the Rez caught you yet?" she said, fishing for information.

Joshua tried to conceal his awkwardness. "Um, no," he responded, purposely not giving her much to form a conversation with.

"Well, that surprises me," she said. "Your dancing sure caught my attention."

"He's not as good a dancer as Mokwa," Little Deer said.

"Well, in all fairness, no one is as awesome as I am," Mokwa agreed.

"Well, I think you'll be up to Mokwa's level in no time," Kiwi said, sounding supportive. Her eyes glistened as she stared hypnotically at Joshua. "I like your green eyes." She interlocked her arm with his and rested her head on his shoulder.

"I told you he had cute green eyes," Mokwa mumbled.

"You know something, Kiwi?" Jenny said, looking deep in thought. "It seems to me that from the way Black Crow looked at you and Joshua dancing together at the powwow, he doesn't know you have broken up." Jenny made finger quotes as she said "broken up." She was clearly irritated.

Kiwi instantly pulled away from Joshua and gazed directly into Jenny's eyes. Joshua relaxed a bit as Kiwi favored a new target.

"Well, I think you should worry about Mokwa and butt out of my business."

Mokwa just sat there with an uneasy expression, as if not wanting to get involved in the approaching cat fight.

"Joshua is my friend. That makes him my business," Jenny responded assertively.

Suddenly, Joshua noticed a very angry-looking Black Crow walk into the restaurant. He glanced around the room as though he were looking for something and immediately fixated on Joshua and Kiwi. He approached aggressively, and Joshua thought he was going to start a fight.

"So this is why you couldn't meet with me!" Black Crow shouted accusingly at Kiwi, garnering attention from everyone else in the restaurant.

"I can date whomever I want," Kiwi asserted.

Black Crow ignored her and gave Joshua a vicious glance.

"And why should you care anyway?" Kiwi said to Black Crow, as if baiting him to answer.

"I do care," Black Crow said, instantly changing his tone from anger to sweetness.

"Well, in that case, maybe we should talk somewhere," Kiwi said agreeably as she got up to go with Black Crow.

Black Crow immediately put his arm around Kiwi, as though she had just been claimed. Kiwi didn't seem to mind. She turned her head back toward Joshua and whispered a parting remark. "Thanks, Joshua. You were perfect." With that, she walked away with her formerly ex-boyfriend.

"I'm really sorry about that," Jenny said. "I hope I didn't ruin things for you."

Joshua felt relieved, though he masked his exuberance. "It's okay," he reassured her. "I'm sure I'll manage to get over her."

"Don't worry," Mokwa said, as he put his arms around Joshua. "You've still got me," he teased.

The night had turned out pretty good, Joshua decided. He'd learned about the Midewin, Mokwa was being extra flirtatious, and Kiwi thankfully was already taken. But most importantly, Joshua realized he was finally warming up to Jenny. She served a useful purpose in shielding him from Kiwi, after all.

TWENTY

IT WAS nearly 9:00 p.m. by the time Joshua got back home from his evening off the Rez. His grandfather was still at the village, so Joshua couldn't talk with him. Questions whirled in his head as he reviewed his conversation with his friends about the Midewin. He fell asleep waiting for his grandfather to come home, and when he finally awoke at 4:00 a.m., he didn't want to bother his grandfather so early. So Joshua took his morning jog and practiced his Fancy Dance by the lake, fully determined to have a long conversation with his grandfather during breakfast. Of course, Mokwa showed up for breakfast, and Joshua wanted to talk with his grandfather alone. So once again, Joshua put off asking about the Midewin. But breakfast was still a good opportunity to bring up the other issue that was bothering him.

"Grandfather?"

"Yes, grandson," Gentle Eagle replied while preparing breakfast for the three of them.

"Why don't I have a name?" he asked.

"I thought your name was Pukawiss?" Gentle Eagle replied instantly.

"Yeah, bro, I gave you that name. Don't you like it?" Mokwa asked, acting offended.

"No, I mean, yes—I love it. That's not the issue," Joshua said, stumbling to enunciate his real concern.

"What is the issue, my grandson?"

"He thinks he's not a real Indian because Black Crow's being a big jerk and crap," said Mokwa.

"I see," said Gentle Eagle.

"It's just that everyone here, I mean, all the real Ojibwe, have a name. And I love my nickname. I just want a real Indian name."

"All names are real names," Gentle Eagle replied. "A nickname is a gift of friendship. It indicates that someone is paying attention to you—that someone knows who you are." Gentle Eagle walked over and placed his special hot cereal on the table for the boys to enjoy. He then continued his thoughts. "You will get many such names as you meet new people—and as you grow and change as a person. Each name is real, and you should be proud of them."

"Yeah, Joshua, that was a valuable gift I gave you," Mokwa said.

"I know, Mokwa," Joshua said gently, to reassure his best friend. "I love the name you gave me. I love Pukawiss. And it fits perfectly." But he was not content with the response. In his mind, he was illegitimate, an apple, as long as he didn't have an official name. "But I need an Ojibwe name."

Mokwa looked over to Joshua and nodded, indicating it was time.

"Now, just like I showed you," he whispered to Joshua.

Joshua pulled out a small pouch of tobacco from his pocket and offered it to Gentle Eagle, who was now sitting next to him eating his cereal. Gentle Eagle stopped eating and graciously received the offering from Joshua. Tobacco was considered a sacred plant to the Ojibwe, Mokwa had taught Joshua. It was often burned in rituals, as it would carry prayers to the Creator. It was the proper gift to give to an elder when making such an important request as asking for a name.

"Grandpa, would you be my name-giver?"

A tear welled up in Gentle Eagle's eye. "Joshua, you have grown into a fine young man. I am honored to be your name-giver. I will pray to the spirits, and I will find your name." Gentle Eagle paused for a moment as if reflecting on their conversation. "I suppose that's the difference," he finally added. "A nickname is a gift from your friends. But your Ojibwe name is a gift from the spirits."

Finally, Joshua would have his own Ojibwe name. There could be no better name-giver than Gentle Eagle. He was part of the Midewin, after all. And if he gave someone a name, then no one could challenge his identity anymore, not even Black Crow. As Gentle Eagle accepted the request, Joshua felt more legitimate somehow.

"So can I have it today?" he asked impatiently.

"Ha, the spirits rarely move that fast," Gentle Eagle said jovially.

"How long, then?" Joshua pressed.

Mokwa chimed in. "It could take days, weeks, even months."

"Months!"

"I'm sure I could pull some strings with the manitous and have it to you sometime soon," Gentle Eagle teased.

Joshua knew the anticipation would kill him. But if it meant getting an authentic name, he decided he would be patient and wait.

"So is there anything I need to do to prepare?"

"Just be true to yourself, my grandson."

"No problem," Joshua said assuredly, even though he didn't quite understand what that meant.

He sat back down and continued to eat his "raccoon guts." Mokwa was almost finished, so Joshua had to catch up with him. His mind turned toward the Midewin, and he realized that now was the time to bring that up as well. He fell silent, and Mokwa seemed to get the hint. "Old Man, I'm heading out early," Mokwa said as he got up to walk out the door. "Later," he added without waiting for a response.

As if Gentle Eagle noticed the scheme, he sat down next to Joshua.

"Is there something else you wanted to talk with me about, Joshua?"

"Grandfather, I've been talking with my friends about the Midewin," Joshua said, deciding a direct approach was best.

Gentle Eagle remained silent as though he hadn't heard Joshua. Joshua could tell that he wanted to avoid this conversation, but he wasn't going to let this go.

"The Midewin," Gentle Eagle repeated. "Well, that's an interesting thing to be bringing up."

"Pastor Martin mentioned them, and so Mokwa told me about them," Joshua continued.

"Mokwa told you?"

"I know that he broke his promise to you, but I can be very persuasive."

"I have no doubt of that," Gentle Eagle said. "You have great power."

Joshua ignored the comment. "So why all the mystery? Why couldn't you just tell me about them?"

"The Midewin are a sacred and secretive group," his grandfather told him. "They are not to be talked about in casual conversation."

"I understand," said Joshua. "But why did Pastor Martin ask if I knew about them?"

"Pastor Martin's motivations are very unique," Gentle Eagle said. "Only he understands his own mind."

"He wants me to come to his church and talk with him," Joshua said.

"Are you going to go?"

"Do you think I should?"

"I think you should do what you feel you need to do," Gentle Eagle said.

Joshua didn't find that very helpful. "So you don't object?" he asked.

"If you're old enough for a name, I think you're old enough to decide who you want to talk to."

"Thanks, Grandfather," Joshua said, gleaming with pride. Now he had just one more conversation to get over with, and the mystery would be solved once and for all.

"But some mysteries should stay buried," Gentle Eagle added cryptically as Joshua got up to leave. Joshua couldn't decide if it was a casual comment or a warning.

TWENTY-ONE

JOSHUA QUICKLY put off his plans to meet with Pastor Martin. Something told him to stay away from that man—a strong intuition of sorts. Every time he thought about it, he got extremely anxious, even feeling a bit nauseous at times. His solution was to bury himself in work at the village.

It was easy to get distracted while at work, as there was always something to do. Joshua especially enjoyed meeting all the new and fascinating tourists who came to visit. Joshua was only fourteen, but when tourists came through his area, they saw him as an expert and treated him accordingly. They also saw him as an Indian, which to many of them seemed foreign and exotic. Joshua felt such pride at the respect and attention the tourists showed him.

But he still most remembered those little kids he had encountered during his first week. They were so young and excited. They had instantly embraced a strange and foreign culture and were captivated by it. If only everyone saw the world with such childlike exuberance, Joshua thought, it would all be so much better. *Why must religion get in the way of everything?* he wondered. And so he avoided the biggest obstacle to that vision and put Pastor Martin out of his mind.

Besides the tourists, Joshua was also excited to meet the new college interns who would finally be arriving. They were supposed to have come only a week after Joshua's arrival, but a mix-up caused them to arrive more than two weeks later. It was a lot of extra work for all the volunteers as a result, but Joshua didn't mind. It allowed him to get to know Little Deer and Jenny better.

While Joshua sincerely looked forward to working with the interns, he had some ulterior reasons for his excitement as well. The interns would be doing a lot of the menial work around the village, thus freeing up time for Joshua to concentrate more on teaching at the Wisdom Lodge.

Gentle Eagle depended on the labor of these college interns. He had connections with a nearby college that agreed to provide the stream of students as part of their environmental education program. In return for their labor, Wiigwaas Village exposed the interns to all aspects of Ojibwe life, just as it was doing for Joshua. Gentle Eagle had tents set up for the interns at a small campsite in the surrounding forest, and the interns provided for themselves as far as food was concerned. So as long as they were ready to work at 8:00 a.m. every morning, it was the perfect deal for everyone.

Gentle Eagle needed to get some things set up at the Trading Post, so he asked Mokwa and Joshua to attend to the interns upon their arrival. Mokwa left the Trading Post when he heard their cars pull into the parking lot. Joshua, of course, followed eagerly behind.

"You ready to have some fun?" Mokwa asked.

"What do you mean?" Joshua replied.

"It's tradition to break in the interns."

"What do you mean, 'break in'?" Joshua asked suspiciously.

"Just follow my lead."

As the two approached the parking lot, they saw four college kids—two guys and two girls—getting their gear from their cars. Heaps of suitcases, duffle bags, and backpacks littered the parking lot. The interns were obviously novices to camping as they had overpacked, Joshua realized.

"Boozhoo," Mokwa said, greeting the new interns. The greeting in Ojibwe was to be expected. But what followed was quite unusual. Mokwa didn't stop with the simple greeting. He continued with a long speech in fluent Ojibwe. The interns just stood there wondering how they were supposed to react. They obviously didn't understand a thing Mokwa was saying to them. That only encouraged him to speed up his speaking pace, while adding an increasingly angry tone. Finally he stopped and stared furiously into the eyes of each intern. Sweat poured down the forehead of one of the guys, and the two girls looked like they were going to try to escape back into the comfort of their cars.

As Mokwa continued to gaze angrily at the interns, he motioned to Joshua, as though it was now his turn.

Here goes nothing, Joshua thought, catching on to the game.

"You've insulted him. He wants to know why you are not responding," Joshua said sternly. He hadn't realized up to that point that he had a real knack for improv.

"Oh, um," one of the young men said. "We don't speak the language."

"Yeah," another college kid confirmed. "But we'd love to learn," he added, plainly wanting to demonstrate respect for their culture.

"You were supposed to learn the language," Joshua replied. "Weren't you told you'd be working in a recreated sixteenth century Ojibwe village?"

One of the girls jumped in, as the guys looked speechless. "Yeah, but we thought we would be teaching in English."

"They didn't speak English here in the sixteenth century," Joshua said angrily. "And we'll be doing the teaching. You'll be working in the outhouses."

Mokwa almost broke character and burst out into laughter, Joshua observed.

"Um, there must be some misunderstanding," one of the guys said reluctantly. "We were told that—"

"Good!" Joshua said forcefully. "So you do know how to do what you're told."

The interns stood there in silence.

"I can't take this anymore," Mokwa said as a smirk finally broke his character. "We were just teasing you. I'm Mokwa and this is Pukawiss. Welcome to the Rez!"

The four interns looked relieved but still cautious.

"Oh wow," said one of the girls. "You really had us going."

"Yeah, you scared me," the other girl said.

"Yeah," one of the guys jumped in. "You were very convincing. Especially with that Mohawk."

Mokwa and Joshua just laughed, allowing the interns to relax a bit more. Suddenly, Mokwa displayed a grim expression.

"What about my Mohawk?" he asked, sounding offended.

"Oh, um, I didn't mean anything by it—"

"Relax," Mokwa interrupted, "I'm just kidding. You guys totally need to lighten up. Now come on and get your stuff. I'll take you to your campsite."

The interns breathed a collective sigh of relief as they reached for their gear. It was obvious they couldn't carry all of their things by themselves. They looked increasingly awkward as they attempted to pick up everything at once, only to have something fall from their arms.

"Do you have a wagon or something that we can use?" one of the guys inquired politely.

"Do I look like a servant?" Mokwa said angrily.

"Ha, you almost had me again," the intern responded.

"I'm not joking," Mokwa said.

"Oh, sorry," the intern said as he frantically lifted up his gear.

"Don't worry everyone, the hike is only a few miles," Mokwa informed them.

It was Joshua's turn to try and contain his laughter. He knew the campsite was only a few minutes away at best.

HAVING A little fun with the interns took Joshua's mind off things for a bit. But he also felt a tad guilty about it, and so he made a concerted effort to get to know the interns over the next couple of weeks and help them better acclimate to this new culture. It got to the point that Joshua didn't want to go back to Gentle Eagle's house after the village closed each night. He often found some reason to stay and talk with the interns, even having dinner with them on a few occasions. After all, Joshua knew what it was like to have to assimilate to a new culture. But he also knew he had an ulterior motive. He was simply avoiding his most pressing problem—having a conversation with Pastor Martin.

Something made him cautious about meeting with him, as though deep down inside he knew he wouldn't like what he learned. Joshua felt cowardly for avoiding his problems and finally decided to open up to Mokwa about it. After all, Mokwa had enough courage to spare.

"You look glum this morning," Mokwa said to Joshua as they arrived at the Wisdom Lodge to await the tourists.

"I've been putting something off," Joshua said.

"So what is it?" Mokwa said. Joshua admired how straightforward Mokwa was about everything.

"You're not afraid of anything, are you?"

"What do you mean?"

"I mean, when you want to do something, you just do it. Like when you confronted the bullies picking on Little Deer, or when you confronted Black Crow."

"Courage is my specialty. We all have our gifts," Mokwa joked. But Joshua didn't laugh, and Mokwa seemed to realize the occasion called for a little more sensitivity. "Look, everyone is afraid, bro. It's about managing your fear, not eliminating it."

"You sound like Gentle Eagle," Joshua observed.

"Where do you think I heard it?"

"It's different with me. I wish I had a bear as my spirit animal."

"Well, I also have a cardinal," Mokwa said.

"What?"

"The bear is my spirit animal, but you can have many spirit helpers throughout your life. When I saw those guys picking on Little Deer, I was terrified," Mokwa confided. "But then I saw this cardinal land in a tree next to me, and it was, like, just staring at me. Mentally, I realized, it was telling me not to be afraid. So then I confronted the bullies. Ever since then, I see this cardinal whenever something happens that requires courage."

Joshua wouldn't have believed it if it weren't for the fact that he recalled the cardinal he saw on Mokwa's shoulder in his dream. Maybe that was his spirit helper. Joshua thought he should probably tell Mokwa about it, but he didn't want Mokwa to think he was weird, or worse, that he was making it all up.

"Whatever, a cardinal, then."

"Tell you what. Next time I see my cardinal, I'll ask him to spend some quality time with you. Deal?"

Joshua smiled. He liked the idea of having a spirit helper look after him. He wasn't sure if he believed it, but still, it helped a bit. And it was just enough to convince Joshua that now was the time to have an overdue conversation with Pastor Martin.

"Thanks, Mokwa," he said.

"No problem," Mokwa replied, visibly clueless as to how he had helped.

"You've got the Wisdom Lodge today," Joshua said as he headed toward the Trading Post.

"Wait, what?" Mokwa responded, confused.

GENTLE EAGLE agreed to take Joshua over to the church and drop him off so Joshua could speak to Pastor Martin. Joshua would have to walk back, though, as the village was still open and Gentle Eagle needed to get back. Joshua felt awkward as he entered the pastor's church, but he didn't know why. He had been raised a Christian, and yet somehow it now seemed alien to him. He had only been joking at the powwow when he informed Little Deer that he gave Christianity up for Lent, but in many ways, he realized, he was also being serious. Joshua had gone to church back in Eagle River, just as his mother expected, but he didn't really believe. And that disbelief started long before his introduction to Ojibwe culture on the reservation.

Joshua credited his turning away from Christianity to his mother's antigay tirades. He especially got irked when she called homosexuality a choice. Joshua knew he hadn't chosen this. And if Christianity got that wrong, he thought, what else might it be wrong about? That question was the seed that would grow into his dismissal of the "one true faith." And now as Joshua walked into the little Baptist church on the reservation, he did so as a stranger to its beliefs, customs, and rituals.

Pastor Martin immediately noticed Joshua as he walked into the church and seemed surprised by the visit. Joshua realized that he had likely given up on seeing him stop by, as it had been a few weeks since their confrontation at the Wisdom Lodge.

"I'm very pleased you came by," Pastor Martin said.

"Thanks," Joshua responded awkwardly.

"Come with me. We can talk privately in my office." Joshua followed him to his office and sat down in a chair in front of Pastor Martin's desk. He was determined to be respectful, as his grandfather had taught him, but at the same time he wasn't going to allow this man to be dismissive of his beliefs.

"So, how should we begin?" Pastor Martin asked. "I know you must have questions."

"I want you to understand that I'm not a Christian anymore, pastor. Little Deer says you don't respect that. And from what I heard, I tend to believe him."

"Joshua, my son, part of you comes from a very ancient and proud culture. I'm not trying to make you ashamed of your heritage."

"I'm not your son," Joshua asserted. He hadn't intended to sound defensive or hostile, but he did.

"Forgive me for being presumptuous, but we are all related. We are all brothers and sisters and sons and daughters of the one true God," Pastor Martin insisted.

"You mean Gitchee Manitou?" Joshua said. He didn't necessarily believe in Gitchee Manitou any more than he believed in the Christian God. But he felt more comfortable with what he was learning about Ojibwe beliefs. And so for this conversation, at least, he was going to play a true-believer, but of a very different faith. At the very least, he thought, it would drive Pastor Martin crazy. That alone was worth the conversation.

"No, not Gitchee Manitou, unless by that you mean our Lord and Savior, Jesus Christ, the one and only son of God—whose teachings are provided freely for all to see in the Bible."

"Well, your God can stay at your church. My God lives outside," Joshua affirmed.

"Did your grandfather teach you that?" Pastor Martin asked suspiciously. "Tell me what else he has been teaching you."

"What do you mean?" Joshua asked, surprised by the question. What did any of this have to do with his grandfather?

"Never mind, Joshua," Pastor Martin said, changing his tone. "We don't need to argue. Gitchee Manitou, God, Christ, it doesn't matter what words we use. They are all the same."

"Really?" said Joshua with disbelief. "Tell me about Pukawiss, then. Where is Pukawiss in your church?"

"Pukawiss?" Pastor Martin repeated quizzically. "Well, I thought I'd heard it all over the years living on the reservation. But I'm afraid you've stumped me. Who is Pukawiss?"

"Pukawiss was a powerful manitou," Joshua said. "Like Nanaboozhoo."

"Oh yes, Nanaboozhoo. Everyone here has heard of Nanaboozhoo. He's quite the character. Kind of like a bumbling superhero of sorts," Pastor Martin said dismissively.

"Pukawiss was his brother," Joshua informed Pastor Martin. "They talked about him just the other day at the powwow. I guess you weren't paying attention."

"I see. And what exactly do you expect the church to say about this Pukawiss?"

"You said you'd tell me about my father," Joshua said, deciding he'd better change the subject.

"And the Midewin," Pastor Martin added.

"My grandfather already told me everything I need to know about the Midewin," Joshua asserted.

An expression of recognition and concern came over Pastor Martin, as though Joshua had just confirmed some dark accusation.

"So, he told you all about them?" Pastor Martin repeated.

"My grandfather doesn't keep anything from me," Joshua said.

"Well, then, you don't really need me to tell you about your father."

"We haven't talked yet about my father. That's why I came to you. What do you know about him?"

"Not 'about' him, Joshua. I knew your father personally. He was a member of my church. I knew him since before he was your age. In fact, Joshua, you remind me a lot of him."

"I'm nothing like my father," Joshua said.

"You're stubborn, brave, bright, and confident—and maybe even a little bit arrogant," Pastor Martin pointed out.

Joshua liked hearing those things about himself. He let down his defenses a bit. But those characteristics didn't really fit his father. At least, not the father he knew.

"So why did my father leave the reservation? Do you know that?"

"Yes, I do. Your father fell in love."

"In love?"

"Yes, with your mother."

"What does that have to do with leaving the reservation?"

"You really don't know, do you?" Pastor Martin asked.

"No, tell me," Joshua insisted, tired of playing this game.

"Your mother was a member of this church for a while, Joshua. She grew up and attended church in Rockford, Illinois, but she used to come up to the reservation as part of a youth group to do missionary work up here. That's how she met your father. And they fell in love."

"So why did he leave?"

"Your mother wouldn't marry your father as long as she believed his immortal soul was in danger. She insisted that he convert to Christianity."

"You mean she forced him to give up everything that he believed in?"

"She believed it was for his own good," Pastor Martin said. "Don't be too judgmental. It's amazing what people will do for love."

"If she really loved him, then she shouldn't have tried to change him," Joshua insisted.

"It's not that simple, Joshua. If you believed someone you loved was going to go to hell, wouldn't you try to change them?"

"I don't believe in hell," Joshua responded.

"I see. Is that also something your grandfather taught you? Like he taught you about the Midewin?"

Joshua started to feel defensive as he responded to the pastor. "You keep saying that. But I have my own beliefs. No one taught me anything."

"You're right, of course," Pastor Martin said. "I apologize if I offended you. But you have to admit that you are learning a lot of new things working at—" He paused, unable to suppress the disdain from his tone, before continuing. "—at that village."

"I'm learning about my other half. There is nothing wrong with that."

"Only if it keeps you from the one true God," Pastor Martin said. "Powwows are fine, Joshua. Celebration is fine. But the Midewin, that's another road entirely."

"I've got to go," Joshua said, feeling very uncomfortable.

"One more thing," Pastor Martin said. "How much has your grandfather told you about the Prophecy?"

"The Prophecy?" Joshua asked, curious at the strange question.

"Yes, the Prophecy of the Fifth Fire?"

"Nothing. Why?"

"Why do I find that hard to believe?" Pastor Martin asked incredulously.

"I guess you just don't have enough faith, pastor," Joshua responded with enough sarcasm to fill the room. With that, he got up and walked out.

"Well now, I thought we were having such a good talk," Pastor Martin shouted, trying to get the last word in.

"No," Joshua corrected. "We were having a talk, not a good one."

TWENTY-TWO

JOSHUA WALKED over to the village after his meeting with Pastor Martin. It was about a twenty-minute walk, most of it on the road through the surrounding forests. He could have run the route in much less time, but he needed some solitude to work things out in his mind.

The conversation he had just had with Pastor Martin really got to him. He never knew that his mother and father had met on the reservation. And he certainly didn't know that his mother forced his father to give up Ojibwe traditions. A lot of things started to click for Joshua. Perhaps it's why his father became so dispirited over the years.

By the time he arrived at the village, Joshua was exhausted. Not only had all the mental wrangling taken its toll on him, but a lack of sleep was starting to get to him as well. He was used to getting up early, but he had been getting up even earlier than normal lately due to his Fancy Dancing by the lake. Joshua's spirit was determined to master Fancy Dancing, but his body clearly needed some rest.

Joshua walked into the Trading Post, where his grandfather was standing behind the counter. He sat behind the counter next to Gentle Eagle, and laid his head on his grandfather's shoulder.

"I'm tired, Grandfather," Joshua said as his eyes started to close. "It's been a long day."

"Ha, it's not even noon yet," Gentle Eagle said, finding Joshua's comment amusing.

Joshua simply mumbled an incomprehensible response. For a second, he felt like he was dreaming again. He recalled the dream about Mokwa in the canoe in the middle of the lake. He could practically hear the thunder from the distant storm reverberate through his entire body.

"I see your early-morning dance practice is taking its toll on you, Joshua."

"What?" Joshua said, coming out of it. "No, it's not that," he replied, his head still comfortably resting on his grandfather's shoulder.

"Why so tired, then?"

"My dreams, I think. They freak me out," Joshua answered quietly, drifting off.

"Dreams?" Gentle Eagle asked. "What have you been dreaming about?"

"I don't know, many things," Joshua replied, his eyes still closed.

"Why didn't you tell me this before?" Gentle Eagle asked, sounding very concerned.

"Because they're just stupid dreams. I have them all the time. I never get any sleep because of them."

"Dreams aren't stupid. They are sacred messages from the manitous," he informed Joshua. "Did you know that?"

"No," Joshua responded, just wanting to drift off into a deep slumber.

"If you have a dream, especially a recurring dream, you should pay attention to it. Someone is calling your attention to something."

"Grandfather, more often than not, they just don't make any sense," Joshua said, starting to get into the conversation.

"The manitous don't always make sense at first. But pay attention and all will eventually become clear," Gentle Eagle advised.

"I don't even know how to start," Joshua said. "They are so weird."

"Do you dream of the future?"

"Sometimes the future, but also sometimes the past," Joshua said.

"You're just like your father," Gentle Eagle confirmed. It was the second time that day someone had said that to Joshua.

"What does my father have to do with any of this?"

"Your father had dreams also—just like you. But he stopped paying attention to them when he got married."

Joshua wanted to change the subject. He didn't want to talk about his father. He decided he wanted to hear his grandfather's take on the conversation he'd just had with Pastor Martin instead.

"Grandfather, Pastor Martin mentioned something about the Prophecy of the Fifth Fire."

"Oh," said Gentle Eagle, sounding intrigued. "What about it exactly?"

"He thought you taught it to me, or something like that."

"I see."

"What is it exactly?" Joshua inquired.

"The Midewin preserve the memory of seven prophecies handed down over the centuries," Gentle Eagle informed Joshua. "Each was handed down by a different prophet. Whenever the Ojibwe people needed guidance, a new prophet would show up to offer them a new vision. The fifth prophet and his prophecy involved a warning that the white men will offer things that will turn out to be false."

"Why would Pastor Martin be worried about it?"

"Some Ojibwe believe that Christianity is that false teaching."

"I would agree with that prophecy," Joshua said.

"Does Pastor Martin know you think that?"

"I probably made that clear."

"And he thinks that belief is coming from me?"

"I guess so, but so what? Mokwa isn't a Christian. Neither is Little Deer. I mean, don't most people on the Rez follow the old ways?"

"Many follow the old ways, and many follow the new," Gentle Eagle said cryptically.

"Well, which is correct—the old ways or the new?" Joshua asked, suddenly feeling confused.

"You must decide that on your own."

"But you decided, and you decided it was the Midewin ways."

"Still, there are more Christians on this reservation," Gentle Eagle said. "They go to Pastor Martin and ask him to pray for them when they have a problem." Joshua listened closely, his head still relaxing on Gentle Eagle's shoulder. "Then, unbeknownst to Pastor Martin, they also come to the Midewin for help and ask for our prayers. Do you understand what I'm saying?" Gentle Eagle asked.

"No," Joshua replied.

"For many Ojibwe, their religious beliefs encompass both traditions," Gentle Eagle continued. "You see, Joshua, we Indians are lucky. Most people only have one religion. We get two for the price of one. That's what it means for many people to be Indian today. Now do you get it?"

"I think so."

"So you must find what is true for you," Gentle Eagle said. "What is true for you, Joshua?"

"Pastor Martin doesn't know about Pukawiss," Joshua said. "There is no place for me with the Christians."

"Then you find a way that works for you. Do Ojibwe teachings work for you?"

"I don't know, Grandfather. I guess I'm still learning."

"So am I," Gentle Eagle snickered.

"I hear about the manitous, and Gitchee Manitou, and it's fascinating," said Joshua. "But they seem like just stories. How do I know that Gitchee Manitou is any more real than the God who speaks through the burning bushes? Sometimes I think I just don't believe in any god at all. I mean, science pretty much answers everything, right?"

"Everything?" Gentle Eagle asked skeptically.

"Well, yeah. I mean, it's given us technology and the cures for diseases and everything. You know?" Joshua looked to his grandfather, expecting him to agree.

"I think science has given people much power," Gentle Eagle said. "But it has not made people happier. That is what I think, Joshua."

"Well, some of it has made us happier," Joshua said.

"Can you name just one thing technology has done to make us happier?" Gentle Eagle immediately added a qualification. "And be sure it is something that has not also made things worse."

"Electric guitars?" Joshua said, not entirely confident of his answer.

"Hmmmm, I think you got me on that one," Gentle Eagle replied, sounding stumped. "So in your search, Joshua, make sure you leave some room both for manitous and electric guitars. I don't think the manitous will mind. They like music."

Joshua smiled. "I guess that's the difference between Ojibwe beliefs and Christianity, then, because my mom sure doesn't allow room for Nirvana," he teased. "Of course, she doesn't like science all that much either."

"Maybe science and the old ways have other things in common, Joshua. Both make predictions," he said.

"What do you mean?"

"I mean your dreams, Joshua."

"I don't like my dreams. Sometimes they scare me," Joshua said.

"Why is that?"

"I don't know. There is this one dream I've been having. There's a really dark storm approaching. It feels scary. I mean, words just can't describe it."

"I see."

"Do you know what the storm means, Grandfather?"

"I wouldn't worry about it," Gentle Eagle said as he put his arm around Joshua. "It means nothing."

"As part of the Midewin, you probably know everything, right, Grandfather?" Joshua asked, deciding to change the subject.

"You're kind of young to know the secrets of the universe," Gentle Eagle said.

"You know the secrets of the universe?" Joshua asked, suddenly getting very excited.

"What I know, Joshua, is that you are too smart for me, and so we are done for now. I think we should keep having these talks, though."

"I'd like that, Grandfather."

AFTER A long day at the village, Joshua finally got to catch up on some sleep that night. Despite his racing thoughts and the intense heat wave, he fell asleep right away. He woke up in the middle of the night feeling hot and sweaty. But he didn't recall having had any dreams. That was unusual, he thought. Just when he was told to pay attention to his dreams, he stopped having them. His life was so crazy. But that was the last thought he remembered before drifting back off into a very deep sleep.

Suddenly, he was back in Pastor Martin's church. At first he thought it was a memory, but then he realized he was dreaming. He saw his mother and the pastor walking into Pastor Martin's office together. His mother looked much younger, Joshua noted. Pastor Martin turned around and kissed her on the lips. Joshua stared at the two in disbelief. His mother looked reluctant at first, but then she put her arms around Pastor Martin and returned the kiss. This time it was much more passionate.

"Can't you see we are a much better fit?" Pastor Martin said as he grabbed her by the shoulders.

His mother said nothing in response.

Joshua instantly awoke from his dream. He got out of bed instinctively and put on his running shorts. The fresh air typically revived him, but he still had the dream on his mind as he headed for the lake. But this time he wasn't following his normal routine. He wasn't jogging; he was running—faster than he'd ever run before. Joshua desperately tried to get the dream out of his head, but it was no use.

Joshua recalled that Gentle Eagle told him not to fear his dreams but to listen to them instead. *They will teach you things*, Gentle Eagle told him.

Joshua arrived at the lake out of breath. He walked over to the water and gazed at the sunrise. And suddenly, the realization he had been running from caught up with him, demanding that he face it.

"He's my father!" Joshua shouted in disbelief and disdain.

TWENTY-THREE

JOSHUA LOST track of time at the lake as he wrestled with the implications of Pastor Martin being his father. *Maybe my dreams are wrong. They have to be wrong*, he tried to reassure himself. But Gentle Eagle seemed so convinced of the power of dreams. Joshua couldn't just dismiss what they seemed to be telling him.

He practiced his Fancy Dance for hours by the lake, hoping to forget his troubles. But every time he got into the dance, thoughts from his dreams brought back the loathsome notion that Pastor Martin was his father. Joshua had finally felt connected to something for the first time in his life, and now it wasn't even real. If he were Pastor Martin's son, then he didn't even have Indian blood in him. Black Crow had called him an apple, but he wasn't even that anymore.

Dancing usually allowed him to focus on the present, to fully immerse himself in the moment. The chanting especially had that effect on him. But this time, the chanting and dancing only magnified Joshua's feelings of inauthenticity, as though this wasn't really his culture anymore.

Joshua didn't realize how long he had been at the lake, reflecting on his disturbing dreams. The sun had long since risen, and nearby campers were stirring from their tents.

When Joshua finally arrived back at home, Mokwa and Gentle Eagle had just finished eating breakfast. Mokwa seemed worried about Joshua and was about to go looking for him, but Gentle Eagle, sensing

Joshua needed some alone time, had convinced him to finish eating first.

"Joshua! Where have you been? Are you okay?" Mokwa said frantically.

"Yeah, fine," Joshua replied in a nonchalant tone, immediately dismissing Mokwa's concerns.

"You're never late for breakfast," Mokwa said, obviously fishing for an explanation.

"I was dancing," Joshua said, trying to ignore Mokwa's persistence. Joshua grabbed some "raccoon guts" and shoved a heap of it into his mouth. He figured if he was chewing, he wouldn't have to answer any questions.

"Yeah, but still—"

"Can we not talk about this?" Joshua asked stridently. His voice was muffled slightly by the food in his mouth.

"Dude, not talking about it is my specialty," Mokwa said, taking the hint. "That's what Jenny says at least."

Even Mokwa's sense of humor wasn't enough to brighten Joshua's mood. Mokwa patiently waited for him to finish his breakfast and then drove him out to Wiigwaas Village to set things up for the day. It was an awkward drive, since Joshua remained silent the whole way. He simply gazed out the window, still lost in his thoughts.

WHEN THEY arrived at the village, Jenny asked Mokwa to work with her all morning. She clearly had something she wanted to talk with Mokwa about, and it would be a good chance for them to spend a little quality time together. Joshua, once again, would run the Wisdom Lodge by himself. He recalled the creepy tourists and how scared he'd been of them. But Joshua didn't care about being alone anymore. He agreed to run it by himself and ran off to the site, not even saying good-bye.

"He's been acting weird," Mokwa said to Jenny.

"Yeah, well, there is a reason for that," Jenny responded. "And it's why I wanted to talk with you alone."

"Jealous of all my quality alone time with Joshua?" Mokwa teased.

Jenny simply ignored the insinuation.

"Listen, haven't you noticed that something was—" She paused for a second before continuing. "—a bit off about Joshua at the pizza place?"

Mokwa wanted to answer "no," but he knew by now that when Jenny asked him questions like that, she already had the one correct answer in mind. His only real option was to listen to it.

"What do you mean?" he asked, figuring he couldn't go wrong with a question.

"With Kiwi?" Jenny said, as though it were obvious. "Seriously, you didn't notice?"

"He seemed to be having a great time," Mokwa pointed out, realizing that it was the wrong answer even as he said it.

"Around you, maybe," Jenny asserted.

"He's my bro; of course he has a good time around me."

"But not around Kiwi!" she said forcefully, making an obvious point. "Joshua wasn't even upset that she was just using him to make Black Crow jealous."

"What are you saying?" Mokwa asked, just wanting to get the confusion over with.

"I think Joshua is a two-spirit," Jenny said calmly.

"Two-spirit? No way." Mokwa chuckled at the notion. "I'd totally know."

"Way," Jenny responded. "And you're too clueless to know anything."

"No, he was just being shy around Kiwi. He'll open up eventually."

"Look," Jenny said. "What typical teenage boy has no interest in the most beautiful girl in Wisconsin when she practically throws herself at him?"

"Yeah, Kiwi is definitely a fox!" Mokwa agreed. He looked lost in thought.

Jenny hit Mokwa on the shoulder. "I'm being serious."

"Ouch, okay, sorry. Me too. This is me being serious." Mokwa molded his face, attempting to clone Little Deer's stoic expression.

Jenny broke out in laughter.

"I can't stay mad at you," she teased. "But really, what about Joshua?"

"Fine, I'll ask him about it. We're like brothers. He'll tell me anything."

"Oh my God, Mokwa, you can't just ask him!" she said as if Mokwa were an idiot.

"Why not?"

"Because he's probably not comfortable with it." Again, Jenny sounded like she was explaining the obvious to Mokwa.

"He did say his mother was crazy antigay," Mokwa recalled.

"There is something else," she said, quieting down a bit.

"What else?"

"You shouldn't flirt with him."

"Oh my God, you really are jealous of Joshua!" Mokwa teased. "You should be," he added, as his facial expression got really serious.

"You really don't get it, do you?"

"Wow, just tell me," Mokwa insisted, tired of playing this game.

"He's got a crush on you."

"No way! Pukawiss is my brother, that's all," Mokwa pointed out, dismissing Jenny's apparent revelation.

"You have no idea how hot you are."

"Well, when you put it that way, I guess it does make sense," he finally agreed.

"So you've got to be careful around him."

"Careful?"

"Yeah, you are such a tease, and you don't even realize it."

"I can't help it."

"I know you can't," she said. "It's why I love you so much."

"Okay, I'll try. Any more insights to share?" he teased.

"Just a command. Stay the hell away from Kiwi!"

"Why don't you tell me to stay away from Joshua?" Mokwa replied.

"Because that's hot," Jenny joked.

"If I stay away from Kiwi, can I still flirt with Joshua?"

Jenny hit him again.

"Ouch," Mokwa said. "Sheesh."

JOSHUA DID his morning routine at the Wisdom Lodge, but like his Fancy Dancing earlier in the day, it now seemed empty to him. It felt illegitimate for him to be teaching about Ojibwe traditions as though they were his own. He tried his best not to let his attitude show, but he thought the tourists could detect something was wrong with him as they came through his area. But he didn't care. Nothing seemed to matter to him anymore.

He was grateful after looking at his watch and noticing it was lunchtime. He headed up the trail to the picnic table by the Trading Post. Mokwa was already there waiting for him, but Jenny was still finishing some things up at the Moon Lodge. Joshua could no longer maintain any pretense of normality. He sat next to Mokwa, put his head down on the picnic table, and said nothing.

"Joshua, please, it's me, your bro," Mokwa explained. "Just talk to me."

What could it hurt? Joshua finally decided. Telling Mokwa couldn't possibly make things worse. "Do you promise not to laugh or think I'm crazy?"

"Are those the only two options?"

"I think so. I mean, I don't know," he responded, looking up at Mokwa. He slammed his head back down onto the picnic table. "Ouch!" he said, still facing down.

"Just tell me!" Mokwa insisted. "I just went through this with Jenny, and now apparently it's your turn to tap dance around the truth. Life would be much easier if everyone just got to the point."

"It's nothing. It's stupid. I've been having these weird dreams, and I can't sleep, that's all," Joshua told Mokwa, finally getting it out of him.

Joshua noted Mokwa's confusion, as though he were expecting something else from Joshua. But Mokwa didn't say anything more about it.

"Dreams. Got it. Go on."

"Do you believe someone can see the future?" Joshua asked.

Mokwa frowned, like he couldn't for the life of him figure out where Joshua was going with this. "You mean like psychics? Dude! Are you saying that you're having psychic dreams?"

"Shhhhh, quiet," Joshua said, feeling very self-conscious.

"What did you dream about?" Mokwa asked, attempting to lower his voice.

"Nothing. I mean, I dreamt about my mother and Pastor Martin."

"That's totally lame," Mokwa said.

"No, you don't understand," he said before pausing to emphasize his next words. "They were together."

"You are the lamest psychic I've ever met," Mokwa replied, clearly amused by Joshua's dream.

"How many have you met?"

"Are you kidding me? They're a dime a dozen on the reservation."

"Really?"

Little Deer and Jenny finally arrived and joined them for lunch.

"Hey, guys, you'll love this," Mokwa said as Jenny and Little Deer sat down at the picnic table. "Joshua is having psychic dreams."

"No way," said Jenny. "What did you dream about?"

"He dreamt about Pastor Martin," Mokwa said.

"That's pretty lame," Little Deer replied.

Joshua smashed his head back down to the table. "Ouch," he said again.

"Dude, you need to stop doing that," Mokwa pointed out as he took a huge bite out of his sandwich.

"It makes me feel better," Joshua murmured, his face pressed against the table.

"I'll make you feel better, sexy," Mokwa teased.

Joshua looked up as Jenny shot Mokwa a raging glance. He simply sighed in response to Mokwa's flirtations and put his head back down.

"Okay, I'm sorry Pukawiss. Tell me what's bothering you about your dream."

"Pastor Martin is my father."

"What!" Mokwa shouted, simultaneously spitting out his sandwich. He finally looked serious.

"So you're not really an Indian?" Little Deer said suspiciously.

"Oh my God, that's terrible! Pastor Martin is your dad? I totally couldn't handle that," Mokwa said, somehow bringing the conversation back to himself.

"Yeah, he'd make you go to church all of the time," Little Deer chimed in.

"And wear a tie," Jenny added, getting into the scenario.

"So you're really not an Indian?" Mokwa asked Joshua.

"Well, I don't know for sure," Joshua said, confused.

"Come on, Pukawiss. It's not that bad. You've still got insanely sexy green eyes," Mokwa teased, trying to cheer up Joshua.

"Mokwa," Jenny sternly admonished, as she shot him an angry glance.

"Hey bro, come on. Is there something else bothering you?"

Joshua couldn't hold it in anymore. He looked up at Mokwa and let it all pour out. This was going to be a deluge, he realized before even saying a word. "Do you mean besides the fact that my mother abandoned me in a strange land I don't understand, and my father ran off to God knows where, and this crazy preacher thinks I worship the devil, and he might also be my dad, and my grandfather belongs to a secret society of medicine men, and, my best friend, who has a girlfriend, keeps hitting on me, and… and I'm having psychic dreams? Do you mean besides all of that?"

"The dreams don't count. Totally lame," Mokwa said.

"Wait, I thought I was your best friend?" Little Deer said to Joshua, looking hurt.

"Ouch," Joshua said as he slammed his head back down on the table one more time.

"Do you want me to get you a pillow?" Little Deer offered.

"Or some aspirin," Mokwa whispered to Jenny.

"Oh, and I dreamt about your cardinal."

"Lame," Mokwa replied.

Not in the mood for being teased, Joshua finally got up to head over to the Trading Post.

"You gotta learn to be more positive," Mokwa shouted to Joshua as he started to walk away.

"Fine, I'm positive that I'm doomed," Joshua responded before disappearing into the Trading Post.

"That's better," Mokwa replied. He turned back to face Jenny. "Well, that went well."

"You are so clueless," she responded in frustration.

Little Deer simply continued to eat his sandwich.

As Joshua walked into the Trading Post, his grandfather was working on another birchbark basket. That task seemed endless to Joshua. He wondered if he should wait and talk to Gentle Eagle after work. But he finally decided he just couldn't put this off anymore.

"Grandfather, I need you to be honest with me about something," Joshua said, feeling completely lost.

Gentle Eagle continued to work on the basket as he listened patiently to Joshua's concerns. "What's wrong, my grandson? Are you still upset about me being part of the Midewin?"

"No, that's not it at all," Joshua said. He contemplated that for a second and then offered, "Actually, that's pretty cool." Not wanting to get distracted, he instantly got back on track. "Was there something between Pastor Martin and my mother?"

"Did Pastor Martin tell you that?" Gentle Eagle asked, looking concerned.

"No."

"Mokwa, then?"

"No, Grandfather, not Mokwa."

"I see. You solve puzzles. You put the pieces together."

"Well, no, I mean, I guess so," Joshua said.

"You can be confusing sometimes, Joshua."

Joshua finally decided just to tell Gentle Eagle about his dream. "I didn't put the pieces together. My dreams did, I guess."

Grandfather stopped what he was doing and looked at Joshua. "I see. You saw the past?" Gentle Eagle didn't seem at all surprised.

"You mean it's true?" Joshua asked, frightened of the answer.

"It's really none of my business to talk about these things," Gentle Eagle said.

"But I already know, so it's okay. Right?"

"I suppose that's true. I just don't want you to think any less of your mother. It was a very confusing time for her and your father. It could ruin Pastor Martin if it came out."

"You mean no one else knows?" Joshua asked.

"Just me, and your father—and your mother."

"Why don't you use this to get Pastor Martin to back off?"

"That would be wrong, Joshua. It's not what the dreams are for," he said, as though instructing Joshua.

"This is what my dreams told me. And you told me to pay attention to my dreams. Right?"

"Maybe I should be more careful what I tell you."

Joshua prepared himself for the obvious follow-up. He had to know the truth.

"Is Pastor Martin my real father then?"

"No," Gentle Eagle said firmly without hesitation.

"Are you sure?" Joshua asked, wanting to be absolutely certain.

"I'm pretty sure."

"Pretty sure?" Joshua panicked.

"Positive, then," Gentle Eagle offered.

"Positive!"

"Positive that I'm pretty sure. Joshua, you are my grandson. Nothing will change that."

"Grandfather, I have to know."

"Know this. Know that I love you. Know that I always have and always will. Know that I will always be here for you. And if that's still not enough, know this—" He paused before adding, "Know that the timing doesn't work out."

"The timing?"

"The timing of the affair and of your birth. You are still half Ojibwe, Joshua."

"I am? Seriously? No joke?"

"No joke, my grandson."

Joshua threw his arms around Gentle Eagle, giving him a tight embrace, which Gentle Eagle eagerly received. Joshua felt as though a giant weight had been lifted from his shoulders. All the feelings of doubt and insecurity, of illegitimacy, melted away in the arms of his warm and gentle grandfather.

Gentle Eagle knelt down and put his hands on Joshua's shoulders. "I have a present for you," he announced.

Joshua looked surprised. "A present?"

"Call it a belated birthday gift," he said.

"What is it?"

"This weekend, I'm driving Mokwa to a competition powwow in Bay Mills, Michigan. I'm taking you with."

Joshua couldn't believe it. He had been excited about seeing a real powwow ever since the small one he'd seen on the reservation.

"Grandfather, that is the best gift ever!"

"That's not all."

"There's more?"

"When we get back, it will be time for your naming ceremony."

"Are you saying you found my name?"

"Yes, that's what I'm saying."

Joshua threw himself at his grandfather again, giving him another tight hug. "Maybe you should have gotten the name 'Bear,' just like Mokwa," Gentle Eagle teased as he returned the warm embrace.

"Thanks, Grandfather," Joshua said as Gentle Eagle held him in his arms.

"You are welcome, my grandson." He paused and held Joshua tighter. "You are welcome."

"Grandfather?" Joshua murmured, still tightly embracing him.

"Yes, grandson."

"I still think my dreams suck."

"Me too," Gentle Eagle said agreeably. "Me too."

TWENTY-FOUR

JOSHUA DECIDED he would join his group of friends back at the picnic table as they finished up their lunch. He felt foolish for letting his dreams get him down so much. He'd wasted too much time obsessing over Pastor Martin. He'd rather spend quality time with his friends.

"Pukawiss!" Mokwa called out when Joshua left the Trading Post. Joshua whistled joyfully as he sat down next to Mokwa.

"What's up?" he asked, delighted to be with his friends.

"Um, we just wanted to see if you were okay," Jenny said.

"Yeah, I'm sorry I didn't take your dreams seriously," Mokwa said. "But it'll all work out for you."

"What do you mean?" Joshua asked innocently. "I'm fine. Let's get to work."

Joshua got up and hummed a tune that was stuck in his head as he skipped down the trail to the Wisdom Lodge.

JOSHUA'S FRIENDS were having a difficult time keeping up with his mood swings. One minute he was deep in despair, and the next he was almost gleeful.

"Was he humming 'Don't Worry, Be Happy'?" Mokwa asked incredulously. "I think he's gone crazy from despair."

"I think I'm going to be sick," Little Deer said.

"Jenny, I think you're going to have to handle this one. He's beyond me," Mokwa said.

"Fine. I have to fix everything around here." Jenny got up and followed behind Joshua, hurrying to catch up to him.

"Are you going to finish your sandwich?" Little Deer said to Mokwa, pointing to the leftovers on his plate.

Just then, a car screeched into the parking lot. Mokwa and Little Deer didn't have to wait for Black Crow to get out in order to know it was him. Only Black Crow drove like that.

"I think we have trouble," Little Deer said to Mokwa, putting on his signature stoic expression.

"Don't worry. I'll handle this," Mokwa said.

Mokwa stood up quickly, eyeing Black Crow as he got out of his car. Black Crow raced angrily over to Mokwa, as if to challenge him to a fight.

"You have a problem?" Mokwa said to Black Crow, wanting to demonstrate that he was in charge.

Little Deer listened and said nothing. "Yeah, I have a problem!" Black Crow shouted back, getting right into Mokwa's face.

Kiwi was with Black Crow, and she ran up and pulled him back to a distance more suitable for civility.

"I hear you're competing in the Bay Mills Powwow this weekend! You knew I was competing there!" Black Crow broke away from Kiwi and shoved Mokwa forward.

"Can't handle the competition?" Mokwa accused.

"Don't flatter yourself," Black Crow uttered with contempt. "You are not competition."

Joshua and Jenny heard the commotion and ran back to the picnic tables, where Mokwa and Black Crow were seemingly locked in combat.

Black Crow immediately turned his attention away from Mokwa when Joshua approached. "I think Apple is the only person here who would be competition for you," he mocked.

"His name is Pukawiss, and he is a better dancer than you'll ever be!"

"Perhaps that name is fitting after all," Black Crow shouted to Joshua. "Pukawiss was an outcast, after all."

"Pukawiss was the creator of the dance," Mokwa corrected angrily. "Now unless you have money for a tour, I suggest you leave."

"This place smells like wannabes anyway," Black Crow said. "We'll settle this at the powwow. Remember, it's a competition powwow, not an exhibition for white tourists. It might be a bit out of your comfort zone."

"I'm not ashamed to dance for tourists or anyone who wants to watch and learn," Mokwa shouted as Black Crow walked away.

"Just be there!" Black Crow shouted back as he got into his car with Kiwi and sped off.

"Remind me to never get into a fight with you?" Little Deer said to Mokwa.

"THAT WAS amazing!" Joshua said, impressed with Mokwa's display of courage. Joshua had never really understood why Mokwa was called Angry Bear before that moment. Black Crow was the most intimidating person Joshua had ever met, but Mokwa faced him down like he was nothing. "How do you do that?"

"Don't ever let bullies intimidate you, Joshua. They're all bark and no bite."

"What if they do bite?" he responded.

"Well, sometimes you have to bite back," Mokwa replied matter-of-factly.

"Mokwa, don't be teaching Joshua to fight," Jenny said, concerned, although she also looked impressed at the way Mokwa had just handled Black Crow.

"Black Crow deserved it for calling my little bro an outcast," Mokwa growled, obviously feeling very protective.

"Well, you're the one who gave him that name," Jenny said.

"I don't understand," Joshua jumped in, looking at Mokwa. "You told me that Pukawiss created the dance and powwows. So why did Black Crow call me an outcast?"

"Pukawiss is also sometimes called 'the Outcast,'" Mokwa informed him. "His father thought he wasted his time observing birds and animals, and not enough time doing important things, like hunting or finding a wife."

"What happened?" Joshua asked.

"Disowned," Little Deer said coldly.

"Yeah, he didn't exactly fit in," Mokwa said. "Didn't I tell you this?"

"But I do fit in," Joshua said. "Gentle Eagle just told me that Pastor Martin couldn't possibly be my father. So I really am part Ojibwe."

"No one here ever doubted it," Mokwa said.

"Black Crow does," Little Deer chimed in.

Jenny punched her little brother really hard on the arm.

"Ouch," Little Deer said. "That one really did hurt."

TWENTY-FIVE

JOSHUA TOOK in everything as his grandfather drove him and his friends to the competition powwow in Bay Mills, Michigan. Little Deer joked that Joshua looked like a dog staring out the car window with his tongue hanging out. But Joshua didn't care. He was intent on enjoying every last minute of the trip.

But they had been on the road for nearly six hours now. Joshua didn't realize the powwow would be so far away. When Mokwa told him it was in the Upper Peninsula of Michigan, he assumed it would only be about an hour or so away, as it didn't take long to hit the Upper Peninsula from the Rez. But Joshua soon realized that Bay Mills was on the other side of Lake Michigan. Joshua didn't know there were any Ojibwe reservations that far away. They called themselves the "Chippewa" on the other side of the lake, Mokwa informed him on the ride over—a bastardization of "Ojibwe."

"How do you get Chippewa from Ojibwe?" Joshua asked perplexed.

"It's easy," said Mokwa. "You simply eliminate the *O* in Ojibwe, turn the *j* into a *Ch*, and then say it really fast."

"Jibwa!" Joshua shouted, thinking he had it.

"No, do a *Ch* sound instead of the *j*," Mokwa corrected.

"Chibbwa," Joshua proudly proclaimed, thinking he finally had it.

"Oh," Mokwa said as he listened to Joshua's mispronunciation. "Then replace the *b* with two *p*s. See? It's simple."

"O-Chippwa," Joshua repeated excitedly.

"Silence the *O*," Mokwa informed him impatiently.

"Silence the mouth," Little Deer added, a bit grumpily.

Unlike Joshua, Little Deer didn't seem at all excited to be off the Rez. Joshua knew he had been to many powwows before as Mokwa's personal helper. Perhaps for Little Deer the excitement of the actual powwow didn't negate the monotony of traveling to them.

"We are here," Gentle Eagle finally announced.

Joshua quickly glanced out the window and noticed a sign reading Bay Mills Community College, with an arrow indicating the direction. The powwow was being held on the grounds outside the college, so Joshua knew they had finally arrived.

As Gentle Eagle parked, Joshua saw cars everywhere. Hundreds of vehicles sat in the parking lot, with many spilling over onto the grass. And it seemed liked hundreds more were still pulling in.

Their car stopped, and Joshua immediately sprang from the vehicle, followed by Mokwa and, less enthusiastically, by Little Deer. Joshua instinctively moved to follow the line of people walking over to the powwow. Mokwa noticed and called to him to stop.

"Bro, all our stuff won't dance its way over there!"

Joshua was so excited to get to the powwow that he had forgotten their car was packed with all their essentials. It would take a while to get everything from the car. Going to a powwow was much like going to a picnic, Joshua decided. In this case, it was a three-day long picnic. But they only planned on staying for one day—for the Fancy Dance competition. Still, every last bit of space in the car was taken up by gear. It was packed with everything they would need—sunscreen, lawn chairs, blankets, and most importantly, coolers filled with food. In addition, Mokwa had all his powwow regalia, which practically needed another car in its own right. Finally, each of them had packed rain gear, just in case the weather got out of hand. Joshua couldn't believe they had fit everything into Gentle Eagle's run-down sedan.

Joshua threw his backpack over his shoulder and used one hand to carry the lawn chairs. Mokwa handed him a cooler for his other hand. Joshua could barely move. He realized that he'd forgotten the most important thing of all—his sunglasses. He put everything back down, pulled his sunglasses out of his backpack, and put them on, quite pleased with himself. He then picked everything up again. He felt like a tourist, but he didn't care. Nothing was going to ruin this weekend for him.

Suddenly, a car screeched into the spot next to them, immediately grabbing everyone's attention. Joshua instantly recognized the older boy driving—it was Black Crow. Joshua couldn't believe it. He knew Black Crow was going to be at the powwow, but with the chaos and confusion of hundreds of parked cars, how did it happen that Black Crow ended up right next to him? Fate was cruel sometimes.

Black Crow got out of his car quickly and slammed the door shut. His face bore an angry scowl, displaying both his determination to beat Mokwa at the competition and his anger at seeing Joshua there. Kiwi had been sitting next to Black Crow, but her exit from the car was much more graceful, as befitting her natural charm and beauty.

"You fit right in with all these tourists," Black Crow finally barked, gazing directly at Joshua. "Nice sunglasses."

Suddenly, Joshua became self-conscious about his lawn chairs, cooler, and sunglasses. He noticed that most of the people getting out of the cars around him and making their way to the powwow were white tourists. Black Crow was right, he decided. He did blend in quite well with them. He didn't know how to respond.

"Shut up," Little Deer finally said. Little Deer always had the perfect comeback, Joshua thought.

"We'll see who the tourist is when the dance competition is over," Mokwa challenged. "I've got Pukawiss on my side, the Creator of the Dance!"

One could detect a nearly pure contempt in Black Crow's facial expression. "You're right. This can only be settled in the arena. I'm content to humiliate you during the dance," he challenged.

Joshua finally understood that this wasn't about the prize money or the glory for Black Crow; it was about honor and dignity. It was about who was more dedicated to the traditions that were handed down to them for generations. Joshua also realized that he had no problem with Black Crow's unwavering confidence or even his irritating arrogance. After all, Black Crow was a very skilled dancer, and everyone knew it. But Joshua hated the demeaning attitude that went along with it. And he knew that was ultimately what motivated Mokwa at this competition. He was determined to humble Black Crow.

Seemingly content that he had sufficiently intimidated Mokwa, Black Crow grabbed the gear from his car. After throwing his regalia over his shoulder, he placed his right arm around Kiwi and led her toward the powwow grounds. He glanced back a final time, as if to indicate she was his. The two soon disappeared into the swarming crowds.

"Well, Joshua, I don't think you have to worry about Kiwi anymore. She seems quite enamored with Black Crow. Hope you're not too disappointed," Mokwa said.

"I'll get over it," Joshua said stoically. He realized he was starting to sound like Little Deer.

"Don't forget, sexy, you still got me," Mokwa flirted. Jenny was on the other side of the car, but she glared at Mokwa as though she wanted to hit him. Joshua didn't understand their relationship at all.

Though he found her a bit weird at times, Joshua had slowly but surely warmed up to Jenny. In his more exuberant moods, he decided he even liked her—like an older sister, almost.

He simply smiled but said nothing in response to Mokwa's flirtations. His mind was on other things. There was so much excitement in the air. He couldn't get to the powwow grounds and experience his first real dance fast enough. He felt so alive.

THE THRONGS of tourists and dancers convened into one long line as they entered the powwow grounds, herding around the multiple tables set up to sell tickets and handle registration. Gentle Eagle paid for all five of them, but only Mokwa actually had to register, which was required of all dancers.

Gentle Eagle often danced at powwows himself, but he had decided to sit this one out to focus on supporting Mokwa.

When Mokwa registered to dance, they handed him a number to hang on his regalia. It was just one more part of the outfit for Mokwa.

All competitors were assigned a number to make it easier for the judges, as well as the spectators, to follow a particular dancer. There were hundreds of people watching the dancing after all, so no one knew anyone by name.

As Joshua entered the powwow, he was overcome by the energy of it all, as well as the sheer immensity of the place. The weekly powwow held on his reservation now seemed puny and insignificant by comparison. As he walked with his friends, his head constantly shifted back and forth—like watching ping-pong—as new and unique sights constantly demanded his attention from all around. He was completely transfixed by his surroundings.

However, it wasn't the strange sights that first caught Joshua's attention; rather, it was an especially enticing aroma. Permeating the entire arena was the characteristic allure of a donut-type smell. Joshua took a deep whiff and closed his eyes, trying to identify the tantalizing odor.

"Mmmm, smell that fry bread," Mokwa said. "Finally we get to introduce Joshua to some homegrown Native American culture."

Joshua had heard of fry bread during his few weeks on the reservation, but he had yet to actually encounter it, let alone taste it. He couldn't wait to try it. Fry bread was essential to all powwows. Nearly every vendor selling food had some permutation of it. At its simplest, it was like a cross between waffles, donuts, and bread. But most vendors got creative with it, offering everything from fry bread sundaes and pies to fry bread tacos. *How could anyone dance after eating all of this amazing food?*

"Between being at a real powwow and eating fry bread," Mokwa said to Joshua, "Black Crow wouldn't dare question your Ojibwe credentials."

Huge tarps were set up everywhere, acting as stores for Native American shopkeepers, some of whom had come hundreds of miles to set up at this powwow. Many of them made their living traveling from one powwow to another, Mokwa informed Joshua.

As Joshua walked from tarp to tarp, he took in the variety of Indian items available. One tarp offered various Native American herbs and teas. Another sold Native American-themed T-shirts and hats. Yet another had Indian jewelry and artwork, like the stuff at Gentle Eagle's Trading Post.

The line of tarps was endless, creating a huge circle about a quarter of a mile around. But as he approached the center of the circle, another type of arrangement became apparent. Tarps were set up to seat the spectators, facing a large open arena. Inside the arena, Joshua noticed many dancers hopping around to the beat of a group of drummers, chanting and banging in perfect synchrony.

"Are we late?" Joshua asked concerned, noticing the dancing had begun.

"There is no such thing as late to a powwow," Gentle Eagle answered.

"Unless you miss the Grand Entry," Mokwa corrected.

"Most of the dancers have been here for hours already," Gentle Eagle said. "Some probably started at sunrise, but it's the Grand Entry that officially starts the activities."

"What time is the Grand Entry?"

"One," Gentle Eagle told him.

"Oh crap," Mokwa said concerned. "I have to get ready!"

"You still have a half an hour," Joshua noted, looking at his watch.

"Dude, it will take me that long to get into my regalia!"

Mokwa quickly made his way to one of the nearby tarps facing the arena, with Little Deer, Gentle Eagle, and Joshua in tow. This tarp was set up to shelter those participating in the dance competition. Mokwa had already torn his shirt off as he approached the cover. Other dancers were likewise busy getting dressed. It was quite a spectacle to watch hordes of dancers frantically trying to put on an array of items, from multicolored, double-bustled feathers, to breastplates, chokers, and ankle bells. It was all quite overwhelming for Joshua.

Little Deer acted as Mokwa's personal assistant, as he had done many times before. Mokwa called out for what he needed, and Little Deer dutifully dug the item out and presented it to him to wear. He helped him attach the more awkward items, like the double-bustled feathers.

Mokwa had not been exaggerating, Joshua noted. Ten minutes into the dressing ritual, the emcee announced, "Will the dancers please line up." It was obvious the Grand Entry was about to start.

MOKWA STOOD in line with the other dancers waiting for the Grand Entry to begin. Little Deer and Joshua followed him just in case he needed some last-minute help. Mokwa wasted no time getting to know the other dancers. Socializing was his specialty, Joshua noted. Mokwa approached each dancer, introducing himself and shaking their hands. He enjoyed getting to know people, and he especially enjoyed running into someone that he knew from previous powwows. After a few minutes of these interactions, Mokwa walked back over to his place in line, where Joshua and Little Deer waited for him.

"Looks like Black Crow and myself are the only ones here from our Rez," he informed Joshua and Little Deer. "But we got some Potawatomi and Menominee neighbors with us," he said excitedly. "Oh, and there is a whole carload of Sioux from South Dakota!" Mokwa added. "Traditional enemies," he said to Joshua. "But these guys are pretty nice."

But most of the dancers Mokwa met were from Michigan, the host state for the powwow. Like Wisconsin, it also had numerous reservations.

"Spectators, take your seats. Dancers, it's time," the emcee said, his voice booming from the many speakers set up throughout the arena.

Joshua and Little Deer ran to a nearby shelter, where Gentle Eagle had set up the lawn chairs. He managed to find a great spot for them, which surprised Joshua considering the size of the crowds.

"Grandfather, how did you find such good seats?"

"I'm an elder," Gentle Eagle reminded him.

Joshua should have known that. Being an elder came with certain privileges. Everyone was willing to give up some space for an elder.

The drumming group began beating the central drum, chanting a traditional song, thus signaling the beginning to the Grand Entry. It was nothing like the one Joshua had witnessed on the Rez. Here, the line of dancers went on seemingly forever. Each danced out onto the arena, one at a time, performing a simple double-step as they processed. The dancers at the very front were the oldest, Joshua noted. There were at least twenty of such elders. They weren't the best dancers, not at their age, but they kept the beat, and the spectators watched them reverently.

As the line progressed forward, the younger dancers finally came into view, and Joshua noticed Mokwa. It was about ten minutes into the Grand Entry before his age group had arrived. Mokwa looked dashing in his colorful regalia. His feathers displayed a wide range of colors, including a deep blue, contrasting sharply with the white and red feathers that dominated his bustles. Mokwa also jingled from all the bells affixed to his loincloth.

Joshua laughed a bit as he recalled how quickly they had dressed Mokwa. But Mokwa looked calm and confident. So too did Black Crow, who was dancing a few steps behind Mokwa. As Joshua watched Black Crow, he was relieved that Mokwa had let him sit this powwow out. As much as Joshua had practiced, he knew he wasn't ready to dance in a competition, certainly not against the likes of Black Crow. Joshua was content to learn from the best, and he observed closely, taking everything in.

JOSHUA WAITED with Mokwa after the Grand Entry ended for the emcee to call the teen category. The competition reversed the order of the Grand Entry, so the wait would not be long. This served the practical and respectful function of allowing the teens to dance in the sweltering heat, while the elders would dance in the relative coolness of the later evening.

Joshua brought Mokwa some fry bread he had just purchased from a local vendor. He'd wanted to wait until the teen competition was over, but he could no longer resist. His anxiety, combined with the enticing aroma, finally overwhelmed his self-discipline. He had a big smile on his face as he handed Mokwa a half-eaten portion of fry bread. His fingers were covered in honey, a sweetener essential for the full fry bread experience.

"I see you found the fry bread on your own," Mokwa chuckled as he accepted the leftover piece.

"It was Little Deer's idea," Joshua said innocently.

Little Deer walked up behind him, but he didn't have any fry bread or honey in his hands.

"Ha, I don't think so," Mokwa teased.

"Teen Fancy Dance, take your places!" the emcee announced. Mokwa's face quickly got serious, and he handed the fry bread back to Joshua. Joshua shoved the remaining chunk in his mouth and chewed quickly.

Finally, it was time, Joshua noted with anticipation. He gave Mokwa a proud look, encouraging him to do his best in the competition.

"Good luck, Mokwa," Joshua said, then turned to head back toward his seat next to Gentle Eagle.

Mokwa stopped him and gave him a big hug, jingling as he did so. "Thanks, my brother," he said. "This one's for you."

Joshua watched intently from the sidelines as Mokwa walked out to his position in the arena. There were fourteen other dancers competing in this category, all standing equidistant from each other in the giant circle. They waited silently for the emcee to start the competition.

The emcee briefly introduced each of the dancers to the audience, noting their name and number, as well as where they were from. As he announced Mokwa, Joshua almost burst out in applause but stopped himself just short of it, realizing everyone else was dead silent.

After the announcements were over, the emcee signaled the judges to walk out onto the dance arena. Joshua noticed that the judges got as close as they could to each dancer, probably so as not to miss a single move.

"Begin!" the emcee finally shouted, signaling the drummers. The thumping was slow and rhythmic, giving the dancers time to warm up, and the chanting was simple but hypnotic.

"*Ay, ah, ay, ay, ah aye.*" The chant resonated from the speakers. The sounds of ankle bells jingling from the dancers' moves added to the rhythmic masterpiece. Mokwa immediately broke into his two-step, only this time he was dancing within a much smaller radius around his central starting point. Slowly the drums and chanting sped up, daring the dancers to keep pace. Mokwa skillfully kept up, anticipating every change and altering his stepping pattern accordingly.

Mokwa appeared intently focused on his dancing. But Joshua saw him glance up once, catching Joshua gazing at him in admiration. The drumbeat picked up again, and the chanting grew louder. Again, Mokwa instinctively kept up with the beat.

The drummers suddenly and unexpectedly pounded three loud thumps on the drum. The contrasting pace was enough to throw several of the dancers off guard. The drummers always attempted to trick the dancers that way, Mokwa had told Joshua, but he had a special move prepared for it. He ducked down and kicked his legs out, while leaning on one hand, before quickly returning to his normal routine as the beat instantly picked up again. It was his signature move, and it always impressed the judges.

As the normal rhythm resumed, Mokwa alternated his feet in the double-step, adding a dose of spinning on his front foot, while extending his multicolored, lace-covered arms outward. It was like watching a tornado through a kaleidoscope, Joshua thought.

Joshua had been practicing his own dance moves for over a month now, and he had gotten quite good at them. But he had never seen anyone do this in full regalia before, along with fifteen other dancers. It was a sight to behold.

As the song approached its end, the drummers beat faster and faster, until the dancers morphed into whirling bundles of frantic energy, desperately attempting to keep up. Joshua noticed one dancer stop completely, obviously overtaken by the speed. The pace seemed to be taking its toll even on Mokwa. He had a pained look on his face, as though something was wrong. But the dance was almost over. Mokwa looked as though he were desperately trying to make it just a bit further. And suddenly, the drummers came to a sudden, dramatic stop with one final thump. The dancers, synchronized to the beat, instantly came to a halt.

"Thank you, dancers!" the emcee shouted. "Please take your seats as the judges tally the results." The dancers, exhausted, meandered back to the competitors' tarp. The judges convened in the middle of the arena to compare notes.

Mokwa limped off the arena behind them, making his way slowly toward Joshua, Gentle Eagle, and Little Deer. Judging by his face, he appeared to be in agony. Joshua wanted to run out to the arena to help, but he thought better of it. He didn't want to embarrass Mokwa.

As Mokwa arrived back under the shelter, Joshua sprang to his feet, immediately put his arm around Mokwa, and helped him to his seat.

"You okay, bro?" Little Deer said, looking concerned.

"What happened?" Joshua prompted, worried for his best friend and brother.

"I think I sprained my ankle," Mokwa said, seemingly trying to conceal the pain. Tears welled up in his eyes.

"Wow, you managed to finish the Fancy Dance with a sprained ankle?" Joshua said, impressed. "I could never do that."

"Indeed," Gentle Eagle chimed in. "It was quite a performance."

Joshua noted a bit of sarcasm in Gentle Eagle's response, especially when he said "performance." However, Joshua promptly dismissed the notion, deciding he had misread him.

"You looked amazing," Joshua said, impressed with Mokwa's skill. He knew Mokwa was one of the best Fancy Dancers around, but after seeing him compete against some of the other best dancers in the Midwest, he understood why.

"Well, I don't think I'll advance to the finals," Mokwa said. "I missed some beats. It was just too painful."

"Didn't look to me like you missed any beats," Gentle Eagle said.

"And the winners are…," the emcee shouted through the speakers.

"This is it!" Joshua said, hushing everyone around him.

"Number eight!" the emcee shouted as the crowd erupted in applause.

Joshua recognized it immediately as Black Crow's number. Joshua had gotten so caught up in Mokwa's dancing that he'd completely forgotten about Black Crow. He hadn't watched him at all during the dance, so he was stunned that he had advanced.

"And the other winner is...," the emcee added as the applause died down. "Number ten!"

Joshua's face lit up in jubilation. He patted Mokwa on the shoulders. "Nice job, congratulations!" Joshua said. "You really showed him."

Joshua was elated. Mokwa and Black Crow would square off against each other in the final round. It was an honor just to make it that far. Black Crow could never dismiss Mokwa again, not with any sincerity, at least. This was the best day of Joshua's life—the best moment, in fact.

"Joshua, I appreciate the support," Mokwa said, "but how exactly am I supposed to dance against Black Crow when I can barely stand?"

"Too bad," Little Deer said, looking a bit down.

Gentle Eagle observed closely as Mokwa explained the situation to Joshua.

"Dude, you can do it!" Joshua insisted.

"No, Pukawiss, I have a much better idea." Mokwa's face lit up, as if a brilliant and devious thought crept into his mind. "You'll go in my place."

Joshua immediately tensed up as he realized what Mokwa had said. "Are you crazy?" he whispered, not wanting anyone to overhear him. Perhaps the pain from his ankle had overwhelmed Mokwa's senses.

"Dude, I taught you, and you've practiced every day. You can do this."

"But I didn't even register," Joshua argued.

"Put my regalia on, and no one will even know it's not me. Help me get this off," Mokwa said to Little Deer as he began taking off his gear.

"Take off your shirt, Pukawiss," Little Deer commanded Joshua.

Joshua was too stunned to fight back.

Little Deer grabbed Joshua's shirt and yanked it off. Immediately, he slapped a breastplate on him and secured it around his chest.

"But you're taller than me," Joshua protested, still allowing Little Deer to dress him.

"So what?" Mokwa insisted. "No one will notice that."

Little Deer sat Joshua back down and yanked his shorts off. He handed him Mokwa's loincloth and motioned for him to put it on. Joshua obediently complied, while mentally searching for more excuses.

"But I... I've never even danced with regalia on before," Joshua insisted. "I feel like I gained twenty pounds."

"Dancers, you have five more minutes to get ready for the final round."

"Oh my God, Joshua. You can do this!" Mokwa asserted confidently. He got up and walked over to Joshua. "My brother, this is your moment. This is your opportunity to prove yourself to Black Crow. Do this, Pukawiss. Do this for yourself. Do it for me."

Joshua couldn't say no to Mokwa, not after that masterful speech. He tensed up as butterflies overcame him. He was actually going to dance in front of all of these spectators.

"Here is your number," Little Deer said, offering Joshua the badge to attach to his loincloth.

"Now let's get your feathers on," Mokwa instructed.

Joshua felt a moment of relief as his mind fed him one last foolproof reason why he couldn't dance.

"But I'm only fourteen," he whimpered as Little Deer and Mokwa began to lead him toward the arena.

"Shut up," Little Deer said.

"Yeah, shut up," Mokwa replied.

Mokwa nudged Joshua out onto the arena, pushing him to walk the rest of the way by himself.

"What about your Mohawk?" Gentle Eagle said quietly, still observing the situation. Up to that point, he had stayed out of the conversation.

"Oh my God, Joshua, get back here. You need a Mohawk!" Mokwa shouted.

"I'm not cutting my hair!" Joshua said, instinctively gripping his head.

Mokwa frantically gazed around the tarp looking for something—anything—that could cover Joshua's head. He grabbed a nearby roach of porcupine quills and handed it to Joshua.

"Here, put this on your head. No one will know you don't have a Mohawk."

Joshua obliged. It fit him perfectly. He stared back at Mokwa and Little Deer, prominently displaying his pouting lips.

"You look just like me," Mokwa said, obviously not really believing it.

"No, Joshua is much cuter," Little Deer said.

"Hey," Mokwa muttered, looking offended.

"Dancers, take your places!" the emcee commanded.

"Now go." Mokwa motioned toward the center of the arena.

Joshua turned around and ran toward his position. He couldn't believe he was about to do this.

"Good luck, Mokwa," Mokwa shouted to Joshua. He sat down in Joshua's seat, his face beaming with pride. Then he heard Gentle Eagle.

"Your leg seems to have gotten better," Gentle Eagle said stoically.

"Oh yeah, um, ouch," Mokwa said back, not sounding very convincing.

JOSHUA STOOD in his designated spot in the middle of the arena, waiting nervously for the competition to begin. He kept expecting a judge to run up to him and expose his ruse. But no one did. Mokwa had been right. With all his regalia on, including the porcupine quills on his head, no one recognized Joshua. In fact, other than his own group of friends, Black Crow was the only person at the entire powwow who even knew him, and Black Crow was standing about fifty feet away.

Joshua had never been so nervous before in his entire life. He felt like such a coward. He shouldn't have freaked out when Mokwa forced him onto the arena. Instead, he let fear overtake him. And that fear was all the excuse his mind needed for his self-doubt to resurface. *Maybe Black Crow is right about me?* After all, Mokwa was never this nervous. Mokwa had challenged bullies twice his age. And then there was Little Deer, Joshua recalled. He was fearless. He mentally reviewed how Little Deer had taken on the three older drunk tourists who had visited the village. Joshua had been terrified of them, but Little Deer stayed calm and collected. Compared to Mokwa and Little Deer, Joshua felt like he didn't measure up. Perhaps he wasn't a real Indian after all. Maybe he was just a stupid, scared apple.

The internal taunts of self-defeat messed with Joshua's sense of time. He felt like he had been standing there for hours waiting for the dance to start, but it had only been seconds. He scanned the audience. He saw Mokwa, Little Deer, and Gentle Eagle sitting there gazing back at him.

This is not going to end well, Joshua thought. And then he heard the announcement.

"Dancers begin!" the emcee shouted.

The drummers thumped the drum, slowly at first, followed almost immediately by the chanting.

Joshua stood there, paralyzed by fear, unable to move. But as he looked over and saw Black Crow begin his dancing, an overwhelming sense of déjà vu overcame him. He had been here before, he realized. Joshua mentally scanned his memories trying to make sense of the familiarity. *Why do I remember this?* And, just as quickly, the answer came to him. He had been here before in his dreams. He had danced before this very crowd, and they had cheered for him at the end. Joshua recalled the powerful elation he had felt from that dream and how it drove him to practice Fancy Dancing all summer. Then the countless hours of practice came back to him. All the mistakes he had made ran through his head and were quickly replaced by the fact that he had eventually overcome them. Then Joshua knew he could do this. He was ready. After all, he was Pukawiss.

Joshua closed his eyes and let the chanting enter him. It reverberated throughout his body, animating his entire being. Joshua was moving. He was dancing.

"Aye ah, eh, aye ah, eh," the chanters sang in sync with the drums. Joshua moved accordingly. He let the chanting guide him and decide for him the appropriate moves. The drummers increased the speed of their beats, and Joshua kept up, perfectly matching their pace.

He started twirling on his front foot, when the drumbeats got fast enough, just like Mokwa had taught him. The drummers varied their speed and beats, attempting to trick the two remaining dancers. This was the final round, after all. But Joshua wasn't fooled. He kept pace. He was totally in the zone, as though he were one with the drumming. It had completely taken him over.

The speed picked up once again, faster than Joshua had ever heard before. He looked like a spinning top as he twirled around and around with his arms extended and his colored laces waving in the breeze. The beat suddenly dropped to one loud thump, and Joshua perfectly nailed it, stopping his twirling and crouching down to thrust his legs out. It was Mokwa's signature move, and Joshua executed it flawlessly. Then the pace immediately picked up again, forcing Joshua back into a frenzied swirl. His body begged him to stop as he breathed heavily and sweat poured down his forehead. Even with all his morning jogs, Joshua had never experienced anything like this before. But he ignored his body and listened to his spirit instead, and it urged him to continue the almost mystical connection he had established with the drumbeats and chants.

Joshua knew it was almost over. He decided he was going to perform his own signature move, the one he had practiced every morning since his dream. He hadn't always executed it correctly during his many practices, but he knew he would get it right this time. He recalled from his dream everyone cheering him in the end. *I can do this*.

And suddenly Joshua sensed that the drums were about to come to a dramatic halt. Anticipating the end, Joshua threw his arms over his head and launched his body backward, executing a perfect back flip and landing standing up right as the final drumbeat signaled a dramatic end to the competition.

It was over. Joshua gazed up at the audience as they erupted in applause. It was a standing ovation, just like he had seen in his dream. Joshua would never forget this moment. He knew he had done the impossible. He had won the competition.

But as he began to catch his breath, he looked over to Black Crow, who was raising his arms in triumph to the cheering crowds. That's when it struck Joshua that something was wrong. The crowds weren't cheering for him. They were cheering for Black Crow.

"And the winner is...," the emcee shouted over the speakers, "Black Crow!" The crowd continued their applause, even louder now.

All Joshua's self-doubt came rushing back, and he stood there feeling like a complete fool. He started to walk off the arena, even before the emcee informed the dancers to exit the arena for the next dance category. Joshua wanted to melt back into the crowds—into insignificance—before he could be humiliated even further.

"Wait!" he heard someone calling him from behind.

Joshua turned around and saw Black Crow running up to him.

"Mokwa," Black Crow called again, trying to get Joshua to stop walking. Joshua realized that Black Crow had fallen for his false identity.

"We got off on the wrong foot," he said to Joshua. "You are one hell of a Fancy Dancer."

"Um, thanks," Joshua said, trying to mimic Mokwa's voice. He reluctantly took Black Crow's hand and shook it.

"No problem," Black Crow said. "You are a credit to our heritage. We have to stick together, you know."

"Um, yes, of course," Joshua said, turning around and hoping to slip away from Black Crow before his true identity was discovered.

"Yes, unlike that fake apple you hang out with," Black Crow called after him. "He is obviously just a wannabee."

Joshua stopped abruptly in his tracks and turned to face Black Crow. An uncontrollable rage possessed him. Joshua felt like he had proven himself. He was done with the self-doubt. He'd danced almost as well as anyone he'd seen, after only a month of practice. He was learning the Ojibwe language remarkably fast. His best friend and mentor saw him as a brother. And most importantly, he was the grandson of a member of the Midewin. Joshua decided he wasn't going to take it anymore. *What credentials did Black Crow have to match any of that?*

"Listen here!" Joshua shouted at Black Crow.

Just then, Black Crow reached forward and tugged the porcupine quills off Joshua's head, revealing his true identity.

"Looks like you got a haircut, Joshua," Black Crow teased, noting his missing Mohawk. "I was just playing with you. You're a pretty good Fancy Dancer for a complete nube. We should practice together some time. I'll show you some moves."

Joshua felt completely disarmed. The change in character paralyzed him, and he just stood there staring. Black Crow finally put his arm around Joshua and walked with him back to the shelter. Just before leaving the arena for good, Black Crow grabbed Joshua's arm and raised it along with his to the crowd. Once again, the crowd erupted in applause. This time it was for Joshua. This time, it was just as he had dreamed.

Mokwa, Little Deer, and Gentle Eagle were all there to greet Joshua as he entered the dancer's shelter.

"I told you that you could do it, my brother," Mokwa said, beaming with pride. He gave Joshua a big, tight hug.

A white tourist stood next to them watching the scene. He snapped a picture of the two friends as they embraced.

"Careful," the tourist said to Mokwa. "You'll crush his costume."

Joshua calmly broke away from the embrace and turned toward the tourist.

"Regalia, actually," he corrected politely. "It's regalia."

Another dancer shouted nearby in a panicked voice. "Has anyone seen my porcupine quills?"

IT WAS nearly 11:00 p.m. by the time Joshua arrived back at Gentle Eagle's house on the reservation. He staggered through the door, barely able to move. He instinctively pulled his clothes off, stripped down to his boxers, and stumbled over to the couch, collapsing on it facedown.

Gentle Eagle laughed. "I've never seen anyone look so tired before," he said to Joshua.

"Eh," Joshua responded, his face down and eyes closed.

"Ha," Gentle Eagle bellowed. "Do you even know where you are?"

Joshua was still for a second, and Gentle Eagle silently walked to his room so as not to disturb him any further. Just before he reached it, Joshua responded to Gentle Eagle's question.

"Home, Grandfather," he whispered quietly. "I'm home."

TWENTY-SIX

JOSHUA AWOKE from a deep slumber, excited that it was a very special day. Today, Joshua was going to receive an extraordinary gift. His very identity would be handed to him in a solemn ceremony. He would still keep his old name, as well as his nicknames, he was told. But his new name would announce his distinctiveness to the manitous and to the Great Spirit. It would define him and give him a place in the universe. It would reveal his true identity to everyone who heard his name. Joshua was so excited that he barely recalled the previous day at the powwow. All he could think about was his upcoming naming ceremony.

Joshua was also excited that it was Monday—a day off at the village. He would not have to go through his normal routine with the tourists. He enjoyed working at Wiigwaas Village, but it was physically draining at times, sometimes emotionally as well. There was still work to do at the village on Mondays; however, without all the tourists present, he could do that work and recharge at the same time. Joshua was looking forward simply to spending quality downtime with his friends all day.

Mokwa wanted to do something special with Joshua prior to the naming ceremony. He convinced Little Deer and Jenny to give him some alone time with Joshua. Intrigued when Mokwa told him this, Joshua excitedly followed as Mokwa led him toward the lake at the village.

"Are we going to go swimming again?" Joshua asked, curious as to why he'd brought him to the lake.

"No, you're too good at that for me," Mokwa said. "I wanted to take you out on the canoe and spend some quality time with my bro."

Joshua was delighted to hear that. He had been wanting to go out in the canoe since he saw it on the first day Mokwa had given him a tour. Joshua had been canoeing before, but this was different. This canoe was made entirely out of birchbark.

Joshua and Mokwa lifted the canoe up and brought it over to the lake. They placed it in the water, with one end still wedged on the beach. Joshua held onto it tight, leveraging it between his legs, as Mokwa got in. Then Joshua pushed off and sat down in the back. The two paddled out to the middle of the lake.

While the sun bore down on them, small puffs of white clouds occasionally provided moments of relief from the sweltering heat. A swift breeze mercifully embraced them every few moments. Mokwa tore his shirt off, hoping to capitalize on the breeze to cool himself off.

But Joshua's mind wasn't on the temperature. He'd decided it was finally time to tell Mokwa everything that had been bothering him. He had come to know Mokwa as his brother, but he couldn't deny he had some very passionate feelings for him. And with all Mokwa's flirting, maybe, just maybe Mokwa felt something back for him. He knew that Mokwa was with Jenny, but perhaps Mokwa was bisexual, Joshua dared to believe.

But at the same time, he realized that maybe Mokwa just liked to be a tease. Either way, he was tired of second-guessing. It was a skill at which Joshua had become all too proficient. He had to know one way or the other how Mokwa truly felt. Earlier in the summer, Joshua couldn't have handled rejection. But with his naming ceremony coming up, he felt more mature, more adult somehow, and he knew he was prepared for anything. However Mokwa reacted, Joshua could accept it and move on with his life. He decided right then and there that he wouldn't leave the canoe until Mokwa knew the whole truth about him.

"I need to tell you something," Joshua said nervously.

"You can tell me anything, Pukawiss. You know that."

Sweat formed on Joshua's forehead. He wasn't sure if it was from the heat or from his anxiety. He reached down into the lake, cupped a handful of water, and poured it over himself, drenching his shirt and cooling off his body. Mokwa noticed and followed suit.

Suddenly, Joshua felt an overwhelming sense of familiarity. This was exactly as he had seen it in his dream. Joshua immediately looked to the end of the lake and up into the sky above the trees, as if expecting to see a storm. But there was nothing. He noticed Mokwa staring quizzically back at him.

"What are you looking at?"

"Oh, nothing, I just heard it was supposed to storm today, that's all."

Mokwa gazed up at the blue sky and laughed. "It doesn't look like it'll storm for months," he said, enjoying the calm breeze and blue skies. "You worry too much."

"Yeah," said Joshua. "I don't know what I was concerned about."

Do it now, he encouraged himself. *Tell him.*

"So what did you want to tell me?"

Finally, Joshua, decided, it was time. "I've been dreaming about this all summer," he said.

"Dreaming about what?"

"About you and me—"

"You and me?"

Joshua lost his courage and immediately diverted the story. "Um, you and me out here on the canoe," he said. "And there was a storm in the distance."

He hadn't intended to tell Mokwa about that particular dream, but it felt good to open up about it. He had already told Mokwa that his dreams sometimes came true, so this dream shouldn't be too much of a shock. And maybe he could use the dream as an excuse to bring up his true feeling about Mokwa.

"I don't see a storm, Joshua," Mokwa said, looking at the sky above the shoreline. "I told you, your dreams are lame."

"Yeah, I guess you're right," Joshua said, a bit confused. He didn't understand how his dream could have seemed so real, yet in actual life, it lacked an ingredient as essential as the storm.

"So was there anything else you wanted to tell me?" Mokwa asked, pressing him for more.

This wasn't the right time, Joshua finally decided. Mokwa wanted to spend some quality time with him on the day of his naming ceremony, and Joshua didn't want to mess that up. He could tell him later that evening instead—right after his naming ceremony. That would be the perfect time, he decided. He would be given his name, revealing his true identity, at which time he would disclose his true self to Mokwa.

"No, nothing more." He breathed a sigh of relief, realizing he had just bought himself some extra time.

So instead of a long conversation, the two ended up canoeing silently on the lake for an hour. Yet it wasn't awkward. It was calm, serene, and peaceful. It was the perfect day.

When they were done, Mokwa informed Joshua that he was to meet Gentle Eagle right there at the lake at 5:00 p.m. That's when his name ceremony would start.

"You mean you won't be here?" Joshua asked.

"I wouldn't miss this for the world," Mokwa said. "Don't worry, all your friends will be here."

They pulled the canoe back onto the shore and walked back to the Trading Post picnic table to meet with Little Deer and Jenny for lunch.

"There you two are," Jenny said as Mokwa and Joshua approached.

"Happy Naming Day," Little Deer said in an uncharacteristically enthusiastic way.

Joshua smiled. "Thanks, Little Deer."

"Yeah, man, this is a big day for you," Jenny said.

"I wish there was something I could do to prepare for it," Joshua said.

"You just need to show up at five o'clock," Mokwa reminded him. "Just like I told you."

"Don't worry about that," Joshua said. "An army of wendigos couldn't keep me away."

"Ha, only Nanaboozhoo could defeat a wendigo, so don't get cocky," Mokwa said.

"Spider-Man versus a wendigo!" Little Deer challenged.

"This again?" Jenny sighed, as though having seen them play this game too many times before.

"Oh wow," Mokwa said. "A wendigo would totally beat Spider-Man in a fight. It would just totally eat him."

"No," said Little Deer. "Spider-Man could use his webs to get away."

"When you say 'versus,'" Jenny pointed out, "it implies a fight. Now you're saying he would just run away. That's not 'versus.'"

"I said he would swing away, not run away," Little Deer corrected.

In important arguments like this, it was those little details that mattered, Joshua noted.

"If Spider-Man shot out a bunch of webbing from his hands, just as he was being swallowed up," he jumped in, "then the wendigo, with all that webbing to consume, would get so big that he'd just explode."

The group stopped their argument and looked at Joshua strangely.

"I think this one is a draw," Little Deer finally said as the other three nodded approvingly.

Joshua finished up lunch with his friends, still in an elevated mood from his canoe ride with Mokwa.

After lunch, Mokwa told Joshua to spend the afternoon by himself. He could go anywhere he wanted to in the village, but not by the lake, as they had to set things up there for his naming ritual. It was a time for Joshua to reflect, Mokwa informed him. Joshua agreed and walked off to the Wisdom Lodge. There was no place that he'd rather spend an afternoon in deep reflection.

JOSHUA'S MOTHER pulled up to the curve in front of Gentle Eagle's house, screeching to a sudden halt. It was exactly 5:00 p.m. She had been driving for seven hours from Rockford. She got out of the car and slammed the door shut, then realized she'd left her keys in the car.

"Shit," she cursed as she reached to open the door to get her keys out. She grabbed them from the driver's seat where they had fallen, but they slipped out of her fingers and dropped underneath the seat.

"God da—" she shouted before stopping herself. She reached down under the seat and finally got hold of her keys. She then slammed the door shut again.

She ran toward the front door of the house, looking frantic.

"Gentle Eagle!" she shouted, enraged.

When she reached the door, she pounded repeatedly on it, alternately shouting for Gentle Eagle and Joshua.

"Damn it!" she cried as she finally ceased knocking. "I know you're in there."

Another car pulled in and parked right behind hers. Pastor Martin got out of the car and ran up to her.

"I knew you'd be here," he said, sounding almost as frantic.

"Of course I'm here! You called me this morning and told me that my son was being taught devil worship by his grandfather! I knew that I couldn't trust Gentle Eagle!" she shouted at him before turning around and pounding on the door again. "Open up!"

"They are probably at Wiigwaas Village," Pastor Martin informed her. "They are always at the village," he added with contempt.

"Wiigwaas Village?"

"Get in," he said to her as he rushed toward his car. "I'll tell you all about it."

The two quickly got into his car. As she reached out to slam the door shut, her purse fell out of her lap onto the lawn, emptying all its contents.

"Goddammit!" she shouted, this time unable to censor herself.

JOSHUA WALKED to the lake at 5:00 p.m., right on time for his naming ceremony. As he approached from the trail, he saw a crackling fire and caught a whiff of the campfire smoke, as well as smudge, a bundle of dried sage used to purify an area prior to ritual. A gentle breeze rolled off the lake.

Joshua first noticed Gentle Eagle standing inside a circle of people, inviting him to come forward. The four people standing in the circle were at opposite points from each other. Joshua knew immediately that this represented the four directions. It was a part of Ojibwe teachings that Mokwa had never elaborated on, but Joshua knew they were important.

Mokwa stood on the western portion of the shoreline. Directly opposite from him, only a few feet away, stood Little Deer, representing the east. Smiling Squirrel represented the north. Joshua was glad to see him there. It was the last direction that caught him off guard, though. Standing there representing the south was Black Crow. Joshua thought it was some sort of joke at first, but the solemnity of the situation assured him that it was not.

Mokwa had told him earlier that Black Crow would be present, but he hadn't truly processed that until now. According to Mokwa, Black Crow himself had asked if he could be there at the ceremony. Perhaps Black Crow felt guilty for the way he had treated him. Joshua could tell that Black Crow was warming up to him at the powwow, after all. But still, he didn't expect this. Joshua appreciated both the gesture and the symbolism. The punk who had called him an apple was now there to witness the delivery of his Ojibwe name from a member of the Midewin. It couldn't be more perfect.

Gentle Eagle beckoned Joshua to approach, inviting him to come to the center of the circle. As Joshua arrived, Gentle Eagle placed his hand gently on Joshua's shoulder and gazed deep into his eyes. In his other hand, he held a smoldering smudge stick of bundled white sage. Such sticks were often used as a means to purify a person or a place prior to a sacred ceremony. Gentle Eagle took his hand off Joshua's shoulder and waved the stick slowly around Joshua's body. Joshua reached for the smoke and pulled it over himself, as if trying to wash with it. Mokwa had taught him how to do that many times during the summer. Joshua enjoyed the soothing smell of sage, as it calmed his spirit and put him in a reverential mood. Gentle Eagle put the smudge stick down into a clamshell and began the ceremony.

"Joshua, my grandson," Gentle Eagle said. "These are your *we-ehs.*" He pointed to his four friends. "They will act as your witnesses and your guides." Gentle Eagle paused for a moment to let that sink in before continuing. "But they are not just guides for today. They will be there for you always. It is a solemn responsibility that they have all agreed to take on." Again he paused before continuing. "Do you understand, Joshua?"

"Yes, Grandfather."

"I have prayed, Joshua. I asked the spirits to reveal your identity." He stopped at that point and looked toward the woods, as though something had disturbed him. But he turned back and looked to Joshua.

"Joshua, your name is—"

"Get the hell away from my son, you devil worshipper!" Joshua's mother screamed hysterically as she ran onto the lakeshore, dragging Pastor Martin behind her.

"Mother, no!" Joshua yelled when he saw his mother running toward him.

She stopped just short of reaching Joshua and stood in front of Gentle Eagle, as if demanding an explanation.

Gentle Eagle gazed indignantly into her eyes before calmly asserting, "What you have done here shows a profound disrespect for—"

But before Gentle Eagle could finish his words, she slapped him on the face. Joshua grabbed his mother by the arms, trying to pull her away from Gentle Eagle, but she was determined to have words with him.

"How dare you! How dare you lecture me about disrespect!" She looked around at the four Indians covered with face paint, standing in the four sacred directions. She then shot a quick glance toward the campfire. Her horrified expression signified that this looked like some sort of satanic ritual, and her son was being inducted into something wicked and sinful.

"You promised me, Gentle Eagle!" she fumed. "You promised me you would not teach him your ways."

"I didn't have to," Gentle Eagle replied quietly. "He found them on his own."

She looked like she was going to slap Gentle Eagle again, but instead she reached for Joshua and grabbed him by the arms. "You are coming with me," she shouted angrily. But as she began to pull him toward the trail, Joshua resisted. He pushed his feet firmly into the ground, causing his mother to lose her grip. He then pulled away from her tight grasp.

"Joshua!" she shouted, as if more surprised by his defiance than his strength. Joshua slipped by her and started to run for the woods.

Pastor Martin grabbed Joshua, preventing him from escaping into the forest. Joshua hadn't seen him standing there behind his mother. He immediately pulled away from the pastor's grasp and grabbed onto his arms with a steel grip. He stared into Pastor Martin's eyes with an intense rage and swung forward with his fist as hard as he could. It caught Pastor Martin right in the face, and he instantly collapsed backward, crashing into the ground. Joshua turned and fled, continuing his course toward the woods.

"Nice shot," Little Deer said, loud enough for everyone to hear.

Joshua's mother didn't bother to help Pastor Martin up. She looked toward the woods as though she were about to dart after Joshua, when suddenly she heard Gentle Eagle shout.

"Stop! You will never find him, and you will get lost!" Gentle Eagle commanded sternly. "Mokwa will find him for you."

Mokwa immediately dashed off into the woods after Joshua.

"Why do you care if I get lost?" she said sarcastically.

"You don't want to push me right now," Gentle Eagle replied, for the first time in his life not living up to his name.

JOSHUA RACED through the woods at top speed, with no destination in mind. He didn't even know in what direction he was heading. All he knew was that he had to get as far away from his mother as possible. But where would he go? How far could he get running through the North woods before darkness hit? How cold would it get that night? Joshua was wearing only shorts and a T-shirt. He wouldn't last long if the temperatures plummeted, as they often did in northern Wisconsin. And if he did make it through the night, then what? His mother would, no doubt, have the police looking for him. Joshua imagined vicious attack dogs roaming the forest searching for him. As he entertained these thoughts, his legs began to slow down. But just as he started to sink into a deep, dark, chasm of despair, he heard Mokwa coming up behind him.

"Joshua! Pukawiss!" Mokwa called as he got closer.

Joshua sat down on a fallen log, not knowing what to do. He put his face to his hands and started to cry.

Mokwa ran up to the log and sat beside him.

"How did you find me?" Joshua whimpered.

"I followed the sound of cracking sticks," Mokwa said.

"You shouldn't have. I'm not going back. Nothing could make me go back to her!" Tears poured down his face. He cried so hard that he had to gasp for air every couple of seconds. Mokwa sat there next to him, holding him, not saying a thing.

To Joshua, it seemed like hours had passed before he ran out of tears, but it had only been a few minutes. He sat there leaning his head on Mokwa's shoulder, occasionally sniffling but not saying a word. Mokwa didn't feed him platitudes about how everything was going to be okay. They both knew nothing was going to be all right. But Mokwa was there for him, supporting him, holding him. That's what Joshua needed at that moment. Finally, after a while, he could contemplate his next move.

"What do I do now, Mokwa?" he whimpered.

"You go back, Pukawiss," Mokwa replied calmly, holding Joshua even tighter.

"No, I can't. I can't go b—"

"Joshua, I'm not going to lie to you and tell you it's going to be easy. But you have to face this."

"How? How could I face her again?"

"With the same spirit that you faced Black Crow. It won't be easy. But you have a special power in you. And that will get you through."

Joshua didn't respond. He thought about his dreams, how they often came true. They had even given him the courage to take on Black Crow at the powwow. They let him see glimpses of what was coming. Perhaps it was all nonsense, Joshua thought for a second. But he couldn't deny his own experiences.

"What if she doesn't let me come back here?" he said. "What if she doesn't let me ever see you again?"

"Pukawiss, not even the wendigos could keep us from seeing each other again."

Joshua laughed at that. Just a few moments before, he was so despondent that he thought he would never laugh again. Mokwa, it seemed, had a very special power as well.

"And besides, you won't be alone. Don't forget, I'm going to tell my cardinal to watch over you for a while."

Joshua smiled. "There was something I was going tell you after my ceremony was over," he said between sniffles.

"You don't have to tell me." Mokwa kissed Joshua gently on the cheek. "I already know." He got up and reached down for Joshua. "Come on," he whispered. "Let's go back."

Joshua began to cry again, and Mokwa held him a few more minutes. Then Mokwa stood Joshua up, his arm still around his shoulder, and guided him slowly back to the lakeshore.

TWENTY-SEVEN

IT WAS 9:00 p.m. as Joshua threw his last bit of luggage into the back of his mother's car at Gentle Eagle's house. Little Deer and Mokwa stood by him, looking helpless. Gentle Eagle had tried to convince Joshua's mother to let him stay one more night and leave the next morning, but she wouldn't budge. She wouldn't even talk to Gentle Eagle. Joshua fumed, knowing how his mother viewed the situation. She was likely running scenarios in her head of the boys sneaking off with Gentle Eagle into the woods in the middle of the night to complete their satanic ritual. She was probably relieved that she had rescued her son in time. As he slammed the back door shut, his mother finally spoke.

"Now get in the car," she commanded, obviously wanting to put the reservation far behind her.

Joshua said nothing. He headed to the car as instructed, almost robotically. But his obedience couldn't mask the underlying pain he was feeling.

"Stop your pouting, Joshua," his mother carped, seemingly annoyed with Joshua's silent treatment. "You're fourteen, so act your age."

Joshua said nothing as he walked around to the front passenger seat to get into the car. His friends were all waiting there for him in order to say their good-byes.

Little Deer made the first move. He put his arm on Joshua's shoulder and gave him a tight embrace.

"I'm going to miss you," he whispered to Joshua, tears welling up in his eyes.

"Me too," Joshua replied, unable to say anything else. He wanted to cry, but he couldn't. He had no tears left in him.

Mokwa hugged Joshua next, but the two had already said their good-byes earlier in the woods. It was a casual hug, but Joshua could feel in Mokwa's embrace a deep and warm affection. Joshua felt loved and protected.

"Good-bye, bro," Mokwa whispered.

Joshua said nothing back. Gentle Eagle had already walked up behind Mokwa, making sure he had his turn to say good-bye. Joshua dropped his backpack and just stared at his grandfather. Immediately, Joshua began to cry again.

"I don't want to go, Grandfather, please. I don't want to go," Joshua pleaded. As this second round of tears began to flow, Joshua found himself once again choking from lack of air. His grandfather ran forward and held Joshua in a tight embrace.

"I'm so sorry, my grandson," he said to Joshua as the two rocked back and forth. Gentle Eagle was crying as he spoke, something Joshua had never seen before. Suddenly Joshua's own pain didn't matter to him anymore. All he thought about was comforting his grandfather.

"I love you, Grandfather," Joshua said. And with that, he got into the car and started to shut the door.

"Wait," Gentle Eagle said. "You forgot something."

Joshua turned around and looked back over to Gentle Eagle, noticing that his grandfather had picked up his backpack. Joshua reached out for it, sniffled one last time, and then got in the car. His mother wasted no time in pulling away. Little Deer, Mokwa, and Gentle Eagle watched silently until the car turned the corner and was out of sight.

"What did you put in his backpack, Old Man?" Mokwa asked.

"A present," Gentle Eagle answered. "Something he'll need at his new home."

TWENTY-EIGHT

IT HAD been a few days since Joshua's mother tore him from his new life. Mokwa had told him he had to face whatever was in store for him, and Joshua was determined to do so with courage. The few moments he'd had with Mokwa in the woods after his interrupted naming ceremony motivated him to view his troubles as obstacles to be overcome. But having a mother who viewed him as a potential Satan worshipper was the mother of all obstacles. Thankfully, Joshua thought, she didn't also know that he was gay.

Joshua's mother had brought him back to her hometown of Rockford. It was as far away as possible from his old home in Eagle River, and more importantly, from the reservation. Joshua felt like he had really moved twice in one trip. In the first one, his mother had taken him away from his life in Eagle River when she brought him to the reservation. But Joshua didn't care as much about that life anymore. He'd never really connected with his friends in Eagle River, at least not like he had with his friends on the reservation. He hadn't realized how trivial his friendships in Eagle River were until he met Mokwa and Little Deer—and even Jenny. Leaving the reservation, not his old life in Eagle River, was what really hurt.

Joshua was living in the cramped apartment of an aunt he only recently knew he had. It was where his mother had been living since she dumped him off on the Rez. His mother had gotten a job in Rockford at the very church in which she had grown up. Pastor Martin had pulled some strings to get her employment there as an office assistant. He had connections at this small Baptist church, as his cousin, Pastor Bob Johnson, ran the place. Pastor Johnson had been the pastor there for decades, and, in fact, it was he who had sent Joshua's mother to the reservation decades earlier on a missionary trip—the trip where she had met Joshua's father. *Full circle*, Joshua thought.

Now, his aunt's apartment was his newest temporary home until his mother accumulated enough paychecks to afford an apartment for her and Joshua. He was appointed a couch to sleep on, as the two bedrooms were for his mother and aunt. Joshua didn't care. He had grown rather used to sleeping on couches.

After a few days at his new home, Joshua woke up early, feeling particularly down after realizing it was time for his morning routine on the Rez, where he would have practiced his Fancy Dancing by the lake. That realization unleashed a flood of old memories, and he started to cry. He recalled first his infatuation with Mokwa. Joshua now felt rather silly about the way he had fawned over Mokwa all summer. He loved Mokwa dearly, he realized, but it was evolving into something truly brotherly. Regardless of the type, it was still love, and Joshua missed Mokwa terribly. He thought of Little Deer and laughed as he remembered one of his last conversations with him about the wendigos. Simple moments like that were often the most memorable.

And, of course, Joshua recalled Gentle Eagle, the only parental figure he had ever truly had in his life. Joshua missed Gentle Eagle, but the connection he felt with him was so deep that he often thought he could feel his presence.

"Oh my God, Joshua, don't act like a baby. Act your age," his mother scolded as she walked into the living room and saw him crying on the couch. It wasn't the first time she'd caught Joshua crying since she had taken him from the reservation. "It's the first day of my new job, and I'm not in the mood for one of your childish emotional breakdowns."

It was all Joshua could take. He had remained silent when she tore him from his friends, from Gentle Eagle, and from his naming ceremony—forcing him to say good-bye to them forever. He had dutifully done all his chores and never complained about them. He even tried to make the best of things by having civilized conversations with his mother. But not anymore. Maybe he'd needed a few days away from the reservation to really understand the true extent of the transgression she had committed against him. But he understood now, and it was a wrongdoing she needed to pay for.

"Mother," Joshua said in a shaky voice.

"What do you want?" she snapped back.

"Fuck you!" he screamed as loud as he could.

He didn't wait for a response. He jumped up, grabbed his backpack, and ran out the door. He didn't know where he was going, but he had to get away from his mother. He grabbed his skateboard from the front porch and made his way down the road. His mother stared at him incredulously as he rode away. A few tenants noticed him on their way to grab their morning papers, but no one greeted him.

After twenty minutes of riding on his skateboard, Joshua noticed a beautiful forested area with a large lake. His aunt's apartment was on the edge of town, so Joshua reasoned he must be a bit outside the city limits. He was glad to know that something so beautiful existed so close to his new home. This could be an oasis for him, he thought.

He carried his skateboard and sauntered over to the lake, walking around it, exploring and reflecting. He thought about how he'd practiced his dancing every morning around the lake on the reservation. Maybe he could do that here, he thought. After all, this lake was an easy jogging distance from his aunt's apartment.

After a few minutes of exploration and contemplation, Joshua found an opening by the lake with a fallen tree that he could sit on. He rested and gazed into the rippling blue water. He was thirsty after all the skating and exploring, and he reached into his backpack and felt around for a bottle of water. As he did so, he found a letter he hadn't noticed before. Perplexed, he pulled it out and instantly realized it was from Gentle Eagle. He frantically opened it and saw that it had very few words. Gentle Eagle wouldn't have had time to write much, Joshua realized, as his mother had rushed him off the reservation too quickly. It read: *This is your name,* followed by several Ojibwe words—words Joshua was quite familiar with. After giving his name, the letter went on, *You must finish what we started.*

Tears of joy welled up in his eyes. He had come to accept the fact that he would never know his Ojibwe name. And, then, seemingly out of nowhere, it was handed to him in a letter. And his grandfather was right. Joshua knew exactly what he had to do. He was in the right place to do it too, surrounded by the natural beauty of this wooded oasis at sunrise.

Joshua put the letter back into his pack, stood up, and slowly walked over to the lake. The sunrise was brilliant, and it perfectly orientated him to the four directions. He raised his hands into the air and faced each direction, subsequently shouting out his name.

"Onwaachige ndishnikaaz!" he announced to the universe. After each shout, he repeated the words in English, proclaiming, "I am He Whose Dreams Come True."

Adrenaline rushed through him as he shouted his name to the four directions, to the powerful manitous who watched over the universe. He was announcing his presence to the cosmos, making it aware of his identity, his location, and that he mattered. And the manitous listened closely to the young dreamer, acknowledging his existence.

But when Joshua finished shouting his name, he realized he wasn't quite done. It probably wasn't exactly traditional, he thought, but he knew there was one more thing he had to do. He got back up and repeated the ritual, this time announcing his other true name to the manitous.

"Pukawiss ndishnikaaz!" he shouted once again to the four directions. "I am the Outcast!" he added in English. The word "outcast" no longer bothered him, and he began to dance. He danced all morning until the sun was high over his head, until his feet could no longer move. As long as he could dance, Joshua decided, he was at home. His place was always with Pukawiss, after all—Creator of the Dance.

EPILOGUE

MOKWA SLAMMED open Gentle Eagle's door the morning after Joshua left and sat down at his normal spot. He was obviously starving.

"What's for breakfast, Old Man?" he shouted, hoping to wake Gentle Eagle up.

Gentle Eagle heard Mokwa and walked out into the living room, looking bemused. He glanced over to the couch, and saw that it was empty save for a pillow and the sheet that Joshua had been using as his only blanket. He noticed some of Joshua's dirty socks still lying on the floor and picked them up. He sighed and walked toward the kitchen.

"I didn't make breakfast yet," Gentle Eagle said as he greeted Mokwa. "I didn't think you'd come by today."

"Why?" Mokwa asked. "A man's gotta eat."

"He does indeed," Gentle Eagle agreed. "I'll throw something together."

"Whatchya got?" Mokwa asked.

Gentle Eagle paused in response to the question.

"Raccoon intestines," Gentle Eagle teased.

A tear welled up in Mokwa's eye. "Well, that's my new favorite breakfast, Old Man," he said, sniffing.

"Mine too," Gentle Eagle said. "Mine too."

Just then the door slammed open. Mokwa and Gentle Eagle instantly looked to the door, half expecting to see Joshua finishing up his morning jog.

"What's for breakfast?" Little Deer said quietly as he walked over to the kitchen table and sat down.

"Oh, it's you," Mokwa said.

"Sheesh, where's the love?" Little Deer responded.

Mokwa put his hand on Little Deer's shoulder. "I'm really glad you decided to join us—paid staff now, even. You are moving up."

"You are indeed," Gentle Eagle agreed.

"So have you decided what you're going to do with the Indian Skills Camp?" Mokwa asked Little Deer. "I know you like to display your crazy-mad archery abilities up there, but maybe you could add some other skills. Maybe axe throwing or something," he suggested. "That would be awesome."

"Actually, I'm going to train some of the college interns to work at the Skills Camp. I'm going to take over at the Wisdom Lodge instead. Tell some stories, you know?"

Mokwa and Gentle Eagle looked at each other and said nothing. Gentle Eagle walked over to them with a big bowl of his Indian cereal. After placing some in everyone's dish, he sat down.

"So, what stories will you tell?"

"Maybe something about Nanaboozhoo defeating a wendigo!" Mokwa offered excitedly.

"No, I don't think so," Little Deer said sullenly.

"Maybe tell about Nokomis and the creation of Turtle Island," Gentle Eagle suggested.

"I don't know," Little Deer said.

"Well, what are you going to tell, then?" Mokwa asked.

"I think that I want to tell them about Pukawiss."

"That's a good story," Mokwa said.

"Yes," Gentle Eagle agreed. "More people need to learn about Pukawiss."

"I miss him," Mokwa said as he started to sniff again. He wiped his eyes and looked over to Gentle Eagle. "By the way, Old Man, you never told us his name. What is Joshua's Ojibwe name?"

Little Deer and Mokwa looked over to Gentle Eagle, eagerly awaiting his response.

"He Whose Dreams Come True," Gentle Eagle said proudly.

Mokwa pondered the name for a bit before chiming in with his thoughts. "I don't know if Joshua would like that," Mokwa said. "He didn't like his dreams."

"I know," said Gentle Eagle. "But he needs to learn to. And I regret I lied to him about them."

"What do you mean?"

"I didn't tell him what the storms meant," Gentle Eagle said. "I didn't warn him."

"Will he be okay?"

"Don't you worry about a thing. He'll be back."

"How do you know?" Mokwa asked, concerned.

"I saw it in a dream."

JAY JORDAN HAWKE spent way too much time in college and holds a bachelor's, master's, and PhD in history, as well as a second master's in Outdoor Education. He loves everything sci-fi, especially *Star Trek*, and hopes to be on the first starship out of here. In the meantime, he teaches high school full time and anxiously awaits the day when he can write full time. His hobbies include camping, reading, running, writing, and attending powwows. He resides in one of the Great Lakes states near the capital of Tecumseh's confederacy. Jay Hawke loves to interact with fans through social media.

Facebook: https://www.facebook.com/jay.hawke
Twitter: @JayJordanHawke
Weebly: jayjordanhawke.com
Goodreads: https://www.goodreads.com/JayJordanHawke
E-mail: jayjordanhawke@gmail.com

The Other Me

Suzanne van Rooyen

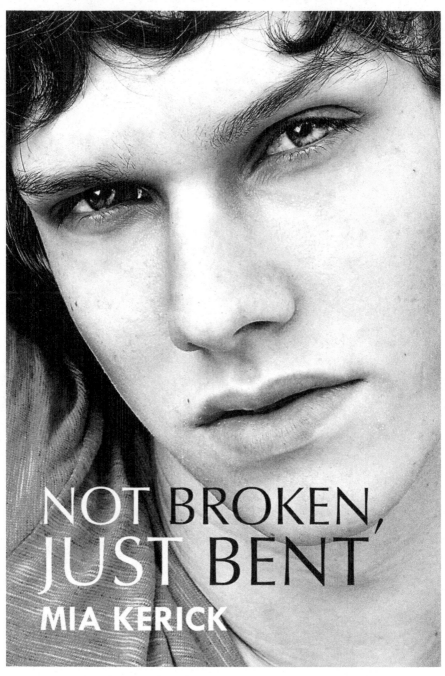

NOT BROKEN,
JUST BENT

MIA KERICK

http://www.harmonyinkpress.com

Also from HARMONY INK PRESS

http://www.harmonyinkpress.com

Harmony Ink

CPSIA information can be obtained at www.ICGtesting.com
Printed in the USA
BVOW08s0051110515

399705BV00008B/166/P

9 781627 986465